SOULSTORM

soulstorm

STORIES BY CLARICE LISPECTOR

TRANSLATED WITH AN AFTERWORD
BY ALEXIS LEVITIN

INTRODUCTION BY GRACE PALEY

A NEW DIRECTIONS BOOK

ACKNOWLEDGMENTS

Grateful acknowledgment is made to the editors and publishers of books and magazines in which most of the stories in this volume first appeared in English translation: *Central Park, Colorado State Review, Exile, Fiction, Latin American Literary Review, Latin American Literature Today, The Literary Review, Liftouts, Ms., New Letters, New Directions in Prose & Poetry, The Ohio Journal, Pequod, Shantih, South Dakota Review, Translation, Webster Review.*

The stories in this volume were originally published in Brazilian Portuguese and included in two collections by Clarice Lispector, *A Via Crucis do Corpo* and *Onde Estivestes de Noite*, both brought out in 1974 by Editora Nova Fronteira, S. A., Rio de Janeiro.

Book design by Sylvia Frezzolini
Manufactured in the United States of America
New Directions Books are printed on acid-free paper.
First published clothbound and as New Directions Paperbook 671 in 1989
Published simultaneously in Canada by Penguin Books Canada Limited

LIBRARY OF CONGRESS CATALOGING IN PUBLICATION DATA

Lispector, Clarice. [Short stories. English. Selections]
Soulstorm : stories / by Clarice Lispector ; translated with an afterword by Alexis Levitin ; introduction by Grace Paley.   p.   cm.   Includes selections from A via crucis do corpo and Onde estivestes de noite. Originally published in Brazilian Portuguese.
ISBN (invalid) 0-8112-1091-1 (alk. paper).—ISBN 0-8112-1091-X
(pbk. : alk. paper)   1. Lispector, Clarice—Translations, English.   I. Title.
PQ9697.L585A6   1989   89-2938
869.3—dc19   CIP

New Directions Books are published for James Laughlin
by New Directions Publishing Corporation,
80 Eighth Avenue, New York 10011

CONTENTS

INTRODUCTION

Clarice Lispector spent the first two months of her life in the town of Chechelnik in the Ukraine. This is a small short fact. The interesting question, unanswered in the places I've looked for it, is—at what age did she enter the Portuguese language? And how much Russian did she bring with her? Any Yiddish? Sometimes I think this is what her work is about. . .one language trying to make itself at home in another. Sometimes there's hospitality, sometimes a quarrel.

Why did they go to Brazil anyway?, an American immigrant Jew provincially asks. Well, a South African cousin answers, since Jews are often not wanted in their old homes, they travel to distant, newer, more innocent places. My mother's best friend emigrated to Argentina. There was a letter from Buenos Aires once. But not again.

Unless Clarice Lispector's parents were linguists with an early knowledge of Portuguese, they must have spoken Russian, as my parents did most of my childhood. It must have been that meeting of Russian and Portuguese that produced the tone, the rhythms that even in translation (probably difficult) are so surprising and right.

It's not unusual for writers to be the children of foreigners. There's something about the two languages engaging one another in the child's ears that makes her want to write things down. She will want to say sentences over and over again, probably in the host or dominant tongue. There will also be a certain amount of syntactical confusion which, if not driven out of her head by heavy schooling, will free the writer to stand a sentence on its chauvinistic national head when necessary. She will then smile.

There are not many smiles in Lispector's work, but they happen in the successful illumination of a risky sentence. You feel that even the characters are glad.

Once you have stood a sentence on its head or elbow, the people who live in those sentences seem to become states of literary mind—they seem almost absurd, but not in a cold or mean way. (There isn't a mean bone in the body of Lispector's work.) But there is sadness, aloneness (which is a little different than loneliness). Some of the characters try desperately to get out of the stories. Others retreat into their own fictions—seem to be waiting for and relieved by Lispector's last embracing sentence.

Lispector was lucky enough to have begun to think about all these lives, men's lives as well as women's, in the early years of the women's movement—that is, at a time when she found herself working among the scrabbly low tides of that movement in the ignorance which is often essential to later understanding. That historical fact is what has kept her language crooked and clean.

In this collection there are many solitary middle-class Brazilian women, urban, heavily European. There are a couple of black cooks, nannies. I thought at one point in my reading that there was some longing for Europe, the Old World; but decided I was wrong. It was simply longing.

It seems important to say something about geography. First Lispector's. She lived for an infant's moment in Russia. Then in Brazil in Recife, then in Rio de Janeiro; then with her diplomat husband in Europe and the United States; then her last eighteen years in Brazil.

Brazil is a huge country. Its population is African black, Indian brown and golden, European white. There are landless peasants. There are the Indian people, whole villages and and tribes driven out of their forest homes by development. There is the vast ancient forest which, breathing, we absolutely require. There is the destruction of that forest continuing at such a rate that a sensible breathing world might be terrified. Imagine living in, being a citizen of a country in which the world's air is made. Imagine the woman, the urban woman writing not about that world but in it. She had to find a new way to tell. Luckily it was at the tip of her foreign tongue.

GRACE PALEY

THE STATIONS
OF THE BODY

EXPLANATION

My editor commissioned me to write three stories which, said he, had really happened. The facts I had, only imagination was missing. And the subject was dangerous. I told him that I didn't know how to write commissioned stories. But—even as he talked to me over the phone—I began to feel inspiration growing in me. The phone conversation was on Friday. I began on Saturday. Sunday morning the three stories were ready: "Miss Algrave," "The Body," and "The Way of the Cross." I myself, amazed. All the stories in this book are bruising stories. And the one who suffered most was me myself. I was shocked by reality. If there are indecencies in these stories, the fault is not mine. It's useless to say they didn't happen to me, my own family, and my friends. How do I know? I know. Artists know things. I just want to tell you that I don't write for money, but rather on impulse. They will throw stones at me. It hardly matters. I'm not playing games, I'm a serious woman. Besides, it was a challenge.

Today is the twelfth of May, Mother's Day. It wouldn't make sense to write stories on this day that I wouldn't want my children to read because I'd be ashamed. So I said to my editor: I'll only publish these under a pseudonym. I had, in fact, already chosen a very nice name: Cláudio Lemos. But he refused. He said that I ought to have the freedom to write whatever I wanted. I gave in. What could I do but be my own victim? I just pray to God that no one ever commissions anything from me again. For it looks as if I'm likely to rebelliously obey, I the unliberated one.

Someone read my stories and said that that wasn't literature, it was trash. I agree. But there's a time for everything. There's also a time for trash. This book is a bit sad because I discovered, like a foolish child, that it's a dog's world.

This is a book of thirteen stories. It could have been fourteen. But I didn't want it to be. It would have shown disrespect for the trust of a simple man who told me his life. He drives the cart on a farm. And he said to me: "In order not to spill blood, I separated from my woman. She had gone astray and had led my sixteen-year-old daughter astray." He has an eighteen-year-old son who doesn't even want to hear the sound of his own mother's name. And that's how things are.

P.S.—"The Man Who Appeared" and "For the Time Being" were also written on that same damned Sunday. Today, the thirteenth of May, Monday, the day of freedom for the slaves—therefore for me, too—I wrote "Day by Day," "Pig Latin," and "Plaza Mauá." "Footsteps" was written a few days later on a farm, in the darkness of the great night.

I've tried to look closely into someone else's face—a cashier at the movies. In order to learn the secret of her life. Useless. The other person is an enigma. And with eyes that are those of a statue: blind.

"My soul breaketh for longing of Thee."

Psalms 119:20

"I, who understand the body. And its cruel exigencies. I've always known the body. Its dizzying vortex. The solemn body."

One of my characters
still without a name

"Therefore do I weep, and my eyes run down with water."

Lamentations of Jeremiah

"And let all flesh bless his holy name for ever and ever."

Psalm of David

"Who has ever seen a love life and not seen it drown in tears of disaster or remorse?"

I don't know whose this is

MISS ALGRAVE

She was vulnerable to criticism. Therefore she didn't tell anything to anyone. If she had spoken, they wouldn't have believed her, because they didn't believe in reality. But she, living in London, where ghosts dwell in dark alleys, knew for sure.

Her day on Friday was the same as any other. It only happened Saturday night. But on Friday she did everything as usual. Yet a terrible memory had tormented her: when she was little, about seven years old, she had played house with her cousin Jack; in grandpa's big bed they both had done everything they could to have little children, but without success. She had never seen Jack again, nor had she wanted to. If she was guilty, so was he.

Single, of course, a virgin, of course. She lived alone in a small penthouse in Soho. That day she had done her grocery shopping: vegetables and fruits. For she considered it a sin to eat meat.

When she passed through Picadilly Circus and saw the women waiting on street corners for men, she practically vomited. Even worse—for money! It was too much to take. And that statue of Eros, up there, so indecent.

After lunch she went to work: she was a perfect typist. Her boss never checked on her, and he treated her, fortunately, with respect, calling her "Miss Algrave."

Her first name was Ruth. She was of Irish descent. A redhead, she wore her hair in a severe knot at the back of her neck. She had lots of freckles and skin so fair and delicate it seemed of white silk. Her eyelashes were also red. She was a pretty woman.

She was very proud of her figure: generously built and tall. But no one had ever touched her breasts.

She usually dined at an inexpensive restaurant there in Soho. She ate spaghetti with tomato sauce. And she had never entered a pub: the smell of alcohol nauseated her whenever she passed such a place. She felt offended by humanity.

She raised red geraniums which were a glory in springtime. Her father had been a Protestant minister, and her mother was still living in Dublin with a married son. Her brother was married to a real bitch named Tootsie.

Once in a while, Miss Algrave would write a letter of protest to *The Times*. And they would publish it. She would note her name with much pleasure: "Sincerely, Ruth Algrave."

She took a bath just once a week, on Saturday. In order not to see her body naked, she would leave on her panties and her bra.

The day it happened was a Saturday, so she didn't have to go to work. She got up very early and had some jasmine tea. Then she prayed. Then she went out for some fresh air.

Near the Hotel Savoy she was almost run over. If this had happened and she had died, it would have been awful, for nothing would have happened to her that night.

She went to a choir rehearsal. She had a melodious voice. Yes, she was a privileged person.

Afterward, she went to lunch and allowed herself to order shrimp: it was so good it even seemed a sin.

Then she took her way to Hyde Park and sat down on the grass. She had brought along a Bible to read. But—may God forgive her—the sun was so savage, so good, so hot, that she read nothing, but just remained seated on the ground without the courage to lie down. She tried not to look at the couples that were kissing and caressing one another without the least shame.

Then she went home, watered the begonias, and took a bath. Then she went to visit Mrs. Cabot, who was ninety-seven years old. She brought her a piece of raisin cake, and they drank tea. Miss Algrave felt very happy, and yet . . . And yet.

At seven o'clock she returned home. She had nothing to do. So she started knitting a sweater for winter. A splendid color: yellow like the sun.

Before going to sleep, she had some more jasmine tea with biscuits, brushed her teeth, changed her clothes, and tucked herself into bed. Her sheer white curtains, she had stitched and hung them herself.

It was May. The curtains wavered in the breeze of this singular night. Why singular? She didn't know.

She read a bit in the morning paper and then turned off the lamp at the head of her bed. Through the open window she saw the moonlight. It was the night of a full moon.

She sighed a great deal because it was difficult to live alone. Solitude was crushing her. It was terrible not to have a single person to talk to. She was the most lonely creature she knew. Even Mrs. Cabot had a cat. Ruth Algrave didn't have any pet at all: they were too bestial for her taste. She didn't have a television. For two reasons: she couldn't afford one, and she didn't wish to sit there watching the immoralities that appeared on TV. On Mrs. Cabot's television she had seen a man kissing a woman on the mouth. And this without any mention of the danger of transmitting germs. Oh, if she could, she would write a letter of protest to *The Times* every day. But it didn't do any good to protest, or so it seemed. Shamelessness was in the air. She had even seen a dog with a bitch. She had been much struck by it. But if God wished it so, then so be it. But no one would ever touch her, she thought. She went on enduring her solitude.

Even children were immoral. She avoided them. And she regretted greatly having been born of the incontinence of her father and mother. She was ashamed of their not having been ashamed.

Since she left grains of rice at her window, pigeons came to visit her. Sometimes they entered her room. They were sent by God. So innocent. Cooing. But it was rather immoral, their cooing, though less so than seeing an almost naked woman on television. Tomorrow, without fail, she was going to write a letter protesting against the evil ways of that accursed city, London. She had once seen a line of addicts outside a pharmacy, waiting their turn for a shot. How could the Queen permit it? A mystery. She would write another letter denouncing the Queen herself. She wrote well, without any grammatical errors, and typed the letters on the typewriter at the office when she had some free time. Mr. Clairson, her boss, praised her published letters highly. He even had said that she might some day become a writer. She had been very proud and grateful.

That's how she had been lying in bed with her solitude. However.

It was then that it happened.

She felt that something which wasn't a pigeon had come in through the window. She was afraid. She called out:

"Who is it?"

And the answer came in the form of wind:

"I am an I."

"Who are you?" she asked, trembling.

"I have come from Saturn to love you."

"But I can't see anybody!" she cried.

"What matters is that you can feel me."

And she really did feel him. She felt an electric shiver.

"What is your name?" she asked in fright.

"Not important."

"But I want to say your name!"

"Call me Ixtlan."

Theirs was an understanding in Sanskrit. His touch was cold, like that of a lizard, giving her goose pimples. Ixtlan had on his head a crown of interlaced snakes, made tame by the terror of dying. The cape which covered his body was of the most painful purple; it was cheap gold and coagulated amaranth.

He said:

"Get undressed."

She took off her nightgown. The moon was huge within the room. Ixtlan was white and small. He lay down beside her on the metal bed. And passed his hands over her breasts. Black roses.

She had never felt what she now felt. It was too good. She was afraid it might end. It was as if a cripple had thrown his cane into the air.

She began to sigh and said to Ixtlan:

"I love you, my darling! my love!"

And—yes, indeed. It happened. She didn't want it

ever to end. How good it was, my God. She wanted more, more, more.

She thought: Take me! Or else: I offer myself to thee. It was the triumph of the "here and now."

She asked him: when will you come back?

Ixtlan answered:

"At the next full moon."

"But I can't wait that long!"

"That's how it is," he said almost coldly.

"Will I be expecting a baby?"

"No."

"But I'll die from missing you! What can I do?"

"Get used to it."

He got up, kissed her chastely on the forehead. And went out through the window.

She began to cry softly. She seemed a sad violin without a bow. The proof that all this had really happened was the bloodstained sheet. She kept it without washing it and would be able to show it to anyone who might not believe her.

She saw the new day dawn all in pink. In the fog, the first little birds began a sweet chirping, not yet feverish.

God lit up her body.

But, like a Baroness von Blich, nostalgically reclining on her satin bedspread, she pretended to ring the bell to call the butler who would bring her coffee, hot and strong, very strong.

She loved him and would ardently await the next full moon. She would avoid taking a bath so as not to wash away the taste of Ixtlan. With him it wasn't a sin, but a delight. She didn't want to write any more letters of protest: she protested no longer.

And she didn't go to church. She was a fulfilled woman. She had a husband.

So, on Sunday, at lunchtime, she ate filet mignon with mashed potatoes. The bloody meat was excellent. And she drank red Italian wine. She really was privileged. She had been chosen by a being from Saturn.

She had asked him why he had chosen her. He had said it was because she was a redhead and a virgin. She felt bestial. She no longer found animals repulsive. Let them make love—it was the best thing in the world. And she would wait for Ixtlan. He would return: I know it, I know it, I know it, she thought. She also no longer had any revulsion for the couples in Hyde Park. She knew how they felt.

How good it was to live. How good it was to eat bloody meat. How good to drink a tart Italian wine, contracting your tongue with its bitterness.

She was now not recommended for minors under eighteen. And she was delighted, she literally drooled over it.

Since it was Sunday, she went to her choral singing. She sang better than ever and wasn't surprised when they chose her as soloist. She sang her hallelujah. Like this: Hallelujah! Hallelujah! Hallelujah!

Later she went to Hyde Park and lay down on the warm grass, opening her legs a bit to let the sun enter. Being a woman was something superb. Only a woman could understand. But she wondered: could it be that I'll have to pay a high price for my happiness? She didn't worry. She would pay all that she had to pay. She had always paid and always been unhappy. And now unhappiness had ended. Ixtlan! Come quickly! I can't wait any longer! Come! Come! Come!

She wondered: could it be he liked me because I am a little cross-eyed? At the next full moon she would ask him. If it were true, she had no doubt: she would push it to the hilt, she would make herself completely cross-eyed. Ixtlan, anything you want me to do, I'll do. Only I'm dying of longing. Come back, my love.

Yes. But she did something that was a betrayal. Ixtlan would understand and forgive her. After all, you do what you've got to do, right?

This is how it went: unable to stand it any longer, she walked over to Picadilly Circus and approached a long-haired young man. She took him up to her room. She told him he didn't have to pay. But he insisted and, before going off, left an entire one-pound note on the night table. In fact she needed the money. She became furious, however, when he refused to believe her story. She showed him, almost under his nose, the blood-stained sheet. He laughed at her.

On Monday morning she made up her mind: she wouldn't work any longer as a typist, she had other gifts. Mr. Clairson could go to hell. She was going to take to the streets and bring men up to her room. Since she was so good in bed, they would pay her very well. She would be able to drink Italian wine all the time. She wanted to buy a bright red dress with the money the long-haired fellow had left her. She had let her hair down so that it was a beauty of redness. She was like a wolf's howl.

She had learned that she was very valuable. If Mr. Clairson, that hypocrite, wanted her to go on working for him, it would have to be in quite a different way.

First she would buy herself that low-cut red dress and then go to the office, arriving, on purpose, for the first time in her life, very late. And this is how she would speak to her boss:

"Enough typing! And you, you fraud, don't give me your phony manners. Want to know something? Get in bed with me, you slob! And that's not all: pay me a good high salary, you skinflint!"

She was sure he would accept. He was married to a pale, insignificant woman, Joan, and had an anemic daughter, Lucy. He is going to enjoy himself with me, the son-of-a-bitch.

And when the full moon arrived—she would take a bath, purifying herself of all those men, in order to be ready to feast with Ixtlan.

THE BODY

Xavier was a fierce, full-blooded man. Very strong, this guy. Loved the tango. Went to see *The Last Tango in Paris* and got terribly excited. He didn't understand the film: he thought it was a sex movie. He didn't realize it was the story of a desperate man.

The night he saw *The Last Tango in Paris* the three of them went to bed together: Xavier, Carmen, and Beatrice. Everyone knew that Xavier was a bigamist, living with two women.

Every night it was one of them. Sometimes twice a night. The extra one would remain watching. Neither was jealous of the other.

Beatrice ate anything that didn't move: she was fat and dumpy. Carmen was tall and thin.

The night of the last tango in Paris was memorable for the three of them. By dawn they were exhausted. But Carmen got up in the morning, prepared a great breakfast—with heaping spoonfuls of thick condensed milk—and brought it to Beatrice and Xavier. She was groggy with sleep and had to take a cold shower to snap back into shape.

That day—Sunday—they dined at three in the afternoon. Beatrice, the fat one, cooked. Xavier drank French wine. And ate a whole fried chicken by himself. The two women ate the other chicken. The chickens were filled with a stuffing made of raisins and prunes, nice and moist.

At six o'clock the three of them went to church. They seemed a bolero. Ravel's bolero.

That night they stayed home watching television and eating. Nothing happened that night: they all three were very tired.

And so it went, day after day.

Xavier worked hard to support the two women and himself, to provide big spreads. And once in a while he would cheat on both of them with a first-rate prostitute. But he didn't say anything about this at home because he was no fool.

Days, months, years went by. Nobody died. Xavier was forty-seven. Carmen thirty-nine. And Beatrice had already turned fifty.

Life was good to them. Sometimes Carmen and Beatrice would go out in order to buy sexy nightgowns. And to buy perfume. Carmen was the more elegant. Beatrice, with her overflowing flesh, would pick out bikini panties and a bra too small for her enormous breasts.

One day Xavier got home quite late at night: the two were desperate. If they had only known that he had been with his prostitute! The three were in truth four, like the Three Musketeers.

Xavier arrived with a bottomless hunger. And opened a bottle of champagne. He was full of energy. He spoke excitedly with the two of them, telling them that the pharmaceutical business which he owned was doing well financially. And he proposed that they go, the three of them, to Montevideo, to stay in a luxury hotel.

In a great hurry-scurry, the three suit cases were packed.

Carmen took all of her complicated make-up. Beatrice went out and bought a miniskirt. They went by plane. They sat down in a row of three seats: he between the two women.

In Montevideo they bought anything they felt like. Even a sewing machine for Beatrice and a typewriter which Carmen wanted so as to be able to learn how to type. Actually she didn't need anything, poor nothing that she was. She kept a diary: she noted down on the pages of a thick, red-bound notebook the dates on which Xavier asked for her. She gave the diary to Beatrice to read.

In Montevideo they bought a book of recipes. Only it was in French, and they understood nothing. The ingredients looked more like dirty words.

Then they bought a recipe book in Spanish. And they did the best they could with the sauces and the soups. They learned to make "rosbif." Xavier gained seven pounds and his bull-like strength increased.

Sometimes the two women would stretch out on the bed. The day was long. And, although they were not homosexuals, they excited each other and made love. Sad love.

One day they told Xavier about it.

Xavier trembled. And wanted the two of them to make love in front of him that night. But, ordered up like this, it all ended in nothing. The two women cried, and Xavier became furious.

For three days he didn't say a word to them.

But, during this period, and without any request, the two women went to bed together and succeeded.

The three didn't go to the theater. They preferred television. Or eating out.

Xavier had bad table manners: he would pick up food

with his hands and make a lot of noise chewing, besides eating with his mouth open. Carmen, who was more genteel, would feel revolted and ashamed. But Beatrice was totally shameless, even walking around the house stark naked.

No one knows how it began. But it began.

One day Xavier came home from work with traces of lipstick on his shirt. He couldn't deny that he had been with his favorite prostitute. Carmen and Beatrice each grabbed a piece of wood, and they chased Xavier all over the house. He ran like a madman, shouting "Forgive me, forgive me, forgive me!"

The two women, tired out, finally gave up chasing him.

At three in the morning Xavier wanted to have a woman. He called Beatrice because she was less vindictive. Beatrice, soft and tired, gave herself to the desires of the man who seemed a superman.

But the following day they told him that they wouldn't cook for him anymore. That he'd better work it out with his third woman.

Both of them cried from time to time, and Beatrice made a potato salad for the two of them.

That afternoon they went to the movies. They ate out and didn't come home until midnight. They found Xavier beaten, sad, and hungry. He tried to explain: "It's just that sometimes I want to do it during the daytime!"

"Well then," said Carmen, "why don't you come home then?"

He promised he would. And he cried. When he cried, Carmen and Beatrice felt heartbroken. That night the two women made love in front of him, and he ate out his heart with envy.

How did the desire for revenge begin? The two women drew closer all the time and began to despise him.

He did not keep his promise but sought out the prostitute. She really turned him on because she used a lot of dirty language. And called him a son-of-a-bitch. He took it all.

Until there came a certain day.

Or better, a night. Xavier was sleeping placidly, like the good citizen he was. The two women were sitting together at a table, pensive. Each one thought of her lost childhood. And of death. Carmen said:

"One day the three of us will die."

Beatrice answered:

"And for what?"

They had to wait patiently for the day on which they would close their eyes forever. And Xavier? What should be done with Xavier? He looked like a sleeping child.

"Are we going to wait for him to die a natural death?" asked Beatrice.

Carmen thought, thought and said:

"I think we ought to figure something out, the two of us."

"What kind of thing?"

"I don't know yet."

"But we have to decide."

"You can leave it to me, I know what to do."

And nothing was done, nothing at all. In a little while it would be dawn, and nothing had happened. Carmen made good strong coffee for the two of them. And they ate chocolates until they were nauseous. And nothing, nothing at all.

They turned on the portable radio and listened to

some poignant Schubert. It was pure piano. Carmen said:

"It has to be today."

Carmen led and Beatrice obeyed. It was a special night: full of stars which looked at them sparkling and tranquil. What silence. But what silence! The two went up close to Xavier to see if it would inspire them. Xavier snorted. Carmen felt really inspired.

She said to Beatrice:

"There are two butcher knives in the kitchen."

"So what?"

"So there are two of us, and we've got two knives."

"So what?"

"So, you ass, we two have arms and can do what we have to do. God directs us."

"Wouldn't it be better not to mention God at this moment?"

"Do you want me to talk about the Devil? No, I speak of God who is the master of all. Of space and time."

Then they went to the kitchen. The two butcher knives were newly sharpened, of fine, polished steel. Would they have the strength?

They would, yes.

They were armed. The bedroom was dark. They struck blindly, stabbing at the bedclothes. It was a cold night. Then they finally were able to make out the sleeping body of Xavier.

Xavier's rich blood spread across the bed and dripped down onto the floor—a lavish waste. Carmen and Beatrice sat down next to the dining-room table, under the yellow light of the naked bulb, exhausted. To kill requires strength. Human strength. Divine strength. The two were sweaty, silent, knocked out. If it had been possible, they wouldn't have killed their great love.

And now? Now they had to get rid of the body. The body was large. The body was heavy.

So the two women went into the garden and, armed with two shovels, dug a grave in the ground.

And, in the dark of the night, they carried the corpse out into the garden. It was difficult because Xavier dead seemed to weigh more than when he was alive, since his spirit had left him. As they carried him, they groaned from exhaustion and grief. Beatrice cried.

They put the huge corpse in the grave, covered it with the humid and fragrant earth of the garden, earth good for planting. Then they went back into the house, made some more coffee, and pulled themselves together a bit.

Beatrice, great romantic that she was—having filled her life with comic-book romances about crossed or lost love—Beatrice had the idea of planting roses in that fertile soil.

So they went out again to the garden, took a stem of red roses, and planted it on the sepulcher of the lamented Xavier. Day was dawning. The garden gathered dew. The dew was a blessing on the murder. Such were their thoughts, seated on the white bench that was out there.

The days passed. The two women bought black dresses. And scarcely ate. When night came sadness fell over them. They no longer felt like cooking. In a rage, Carmen, the hotheaded one, tore up the book of recipes in French. She kept the one in Spanish: you never know when you might need it again.

Beatrice took over the cooking. They both ate and drank in silence. The stalk of red roses seemed to have taken hold. Good planter's hands, good prosperous earth. Everything was working out.

And so the story would have ended.

But it so happened that Xavier's secretary found his boss's long absence strange. There were important papers to be signed. Since Xavier's house had no telephone, he went there himself. The house seemed bathed in "mala suerte," evil fortune. The two women told him that Xavier had gone on a trip, that he had gone to Montevideo. The secretary didn't much believe them, but behaved as if he swallowed the story.

The following week the secretary went to the police. With the police you don't play games. At first they didn't want to believe his story. But, in the face of the secretary's insistence, they lazily decided to order the polygamist's house searched. All in vain: no trace of Xavier.

Then Carmen spoke:

"Xavier is in the garden."

"In the garden? Doing what?"

"Only God knows."

"But we didn't see anything or anybody."

They went out to the garden: Carmen, Beatrice, the secretary named Albert, two policemen, and two other men whose identities are unknown. Seven people. Then Beatrice, without a tear in her eye, showed them the flowering grave. Three men opened the grave, ruining the stalk of roses, which suffered this human brutality for no reason at all.

And they saw Xavier. He was horrible, deformed, already half eaten away by worms, with his eyes open.

"And now?" said one of the policemen.

"And now we arrest the two women."

"But," said Carmen, "let us be in the same cell."

"Look," said one of the policemen, right in front of the astonished secretary, "it's best to pretend that nothing at all happened, otherwise there will be lots of noise, lots of paper work, lots of gossip."

"You two," said the other policeman, "pack your bags and go and live in Montevideo. And don't bother us anymore."

The two women said thank you very much.

And Xavier didn't say anything. For, in fact, he had nothing to say.

THE WAY OF THE CROSS

Maria das Dores was scared. But really scared!

It began when her period didn't come. This surprised her because she was very regular.

More than two months passed, but nothing happened. She went to a gynecologist. She diagnosed a clear-cut pregnancy.

"It can't be!" screamed Maria das Dores.

"Why not? Aren't you married?"

"I am, but I'm a virgin, my husband has never touched me. First of all because he's a patient man and secondly because he's already half impotent."

The gynecologist tried to argue:

"Who knows, maybe one night you . . ."

"Never! Absolutely never!"

"In that case," concluded the gynecologist, "I don't know how to explain it. You are already at the end of the third month."

Maria das Dores left the doctor's office with her head spinning. She had to stop at a restaurant and have some coffee. In order to be able to understand.

What was happening? A great anguish took hold of her. But she left the restaurant somewhat calmer.

Walking home she bought a tiny jacket for the baby. Blue, because she was sure it would be a boy. What name should she give him? There was only one name she could give him: Jesus.

At home she found her husband in his slippers, reading the newspaper. She told him what had happened. The man was startled:

"Then I'm St. Joseph?"

"You are," was the laconic response.

They both fell into deep thought.

Maria das Dores sent the maid to buy the vitamins which the gynecologist had prescribed. They were for the good of her son.

Her divine son. She had been chosen by God to give to the world the new Messiah.

She bought a blue cradle. She began to knit little jackets and to make soft diapers.

Meanwhile her belly grew. The foetus was energetic: it kicked violently. Sometimes she would call St. Joseph to put his hand on her belly and feel the son living so forcefully within.

St. Joseph's eyes would then fill with tears. It was going to be a vigorous Jesus. She felt filled with light.

Maria das Dores told the entire awe-inspiring story to her closest friend. She also was startled:

"Maria das Dores, but what a privileged destiny you have!"

"Privileged, yes," sighed Maria das Dores. "But what can I do to prevent my son from following the way of the cross?"

"Pray," advised the friend, "pray a lot."

And Maria das Dores began to believe in miracles. Once she thought she saw the Virgin Mary standing at her side, smiling at her. Another time, she herself performed the miracle: her husband had an open wound on his leg, Maria das Dores kissed the wound—the following day it was gone without a trace.

It was getting cold, it was the month of July. In October the child would be born.

But where could they find a stable? Only if they were on a farm out in the countryside of Minas Gerais. So they decided to go to Aunt Mininha's farm.

What worried her was that the child would not be born on the twenty-fifth of December.

She went to Church every day, and even with her swollen belly she remained kneeling for hours. For the child's godmother she chose the Virgin Mary. And for godfather, Christ.

And so the time passed. Maria das Dores had gotten barbarously fat and had strange desires. Such as wanting to eat frozen grapes. St. Joseph went with her to the farm. And there he continued his cabinet-making.

One day Maria das Dores stuffed herself too much— she threw up and cried. And she thought: the way of the cross of my sacred son has begun.

But it seemed to her that if she left the child with the name of Jesus he would be crucified upon reaching manhood. It would be better to give him the name Emmanuel. A simple name. A good name.

She awaited Emmanuel seated beneath a jaboticaba tree. And she thought: "When the hour comes, I won't scream, I'll only say—Oh, Jesus!"

And she ate the jaboticaba cherries. She stuffed herself, the mother of Jesus.

The aunt, in on it all, decorated the room with blue curtains. The stable was there with its good smell of manure and its cows.

At night Maria das Dores looked up at the starry heavens in search of the guiding star. Who would be the three Magi? Who would bring him myrrh and frankincense?

She took long strolls because the doctor had recommended that she walk a lot. St. Joseph let his graying beard grow, and his hair reached down to his shoulders.

It was difficult to wait. Time didn't pass. For breakfast the aunt made them little cakes which crumbled in their mouths. And the cold left them with hard, red hands.

At night they lit the fire and sat around it warming themselves. St. Joseph found himself a shepherd's crook. And, as he didn't change his clothes, he gave off a suffocating smell. His tunic was of cheap cotton tow. He drank wine next to the fireplace. Maria das Dores drank thick white milk, with a rosary in her hand.

Bright and early she went to check on the cows in the stable. The cows mooed. Maria das Dores smiled at them. All were humble: the cows and the woman. Maria das Dores was on the point of crying. She arranged the straw on the ground, preparing a place where she could lie down when the hour came. The hour of illumination.

St. Joseph, with his shepherd's crook, went to meditate on the mountain. The aunt prepared roast pork, and everybody ate like mad. And the baby did nothing about arriving.

Until one night, at three in the morning, Maria das Dores felt the first pain. She lit the night lamp, woke St. Joseph, woke the aunt. They got dressed. And with a torch lighting the path, they made their way through the trees towards the stable. A huge star sparkled in the black sky.

The cows, awakened, became uneasy and began to moo.

Shortly, the pain came again. Maria das Dores bit her own hand in order not to scream. And the dawn wouldn't come.

St. Joseph was trembling with cold. Maria das Dores, lying on the straw, under a blanket, was waiting.

Then came a really sharp pain. "Oh, Jesus," moaned Maria das Dores. "Oh, Jesus," the cows seemed to moo.

The stars in the sky.

Then it happened.

Emmanuel was born.

And the stable seemed filled with light.

It was a strong and beautiful boy, who gave forth a bellow into the early morning air.

St. Joseph cut the umbilical cord. And the mother smiled. The aunt cried.

Nobody knows if this child had to go the way of the cross. The way all go.

THE MAN WHO APPEARED

It was Saturday afternoon, around six o'clock. Going on seven. I went down to buy some Coca-Cola and cigarettes. I crossed the street and headed for the little shop of Manuel, the Portuguese.

While I was waiting to be helped, a man playing a small harmonica approached, looked at me, played a little tune, and spoke my name. He said that he had known me at the Cultura Inglesa, where I had, in fact, studied for two or three months. He said to me:

"Don't be afraid of me."

I answered:

"I'm not afraid. What's your name?"

He answered with a sad smile, in English: "What difference does a name make?"

He said to Manuel:

"The only person in here superior to me is this woman, because she writes and I don't."

Manuel didn't blink an eye. The man was completely drunk. I picked up my things and was leaving when he said:

"May I have the honor of carrying the bottle and the cigarettes?"

I handed what I had bought over to him. At the door to my building, I took the Coca-Cola and the cigarettes. He stood motionless before me. Then, finding his face very familiar, I once again asked him his name.

"I'm Claudio."

"Claudio who?"

"Well listen to that: who who? My name's Claudio Brito . . ."

"Claudio," I shouted. "Oh my God, please come on up with me to my place!"

"What floor are you on?"

I gave him my floor and apartment number. He said that he was going to pay his bill at the little shop and would then come up.

A friend of mine had dropped by. I told her what had happened and said: "He might be too ashamed to come."

My friend said: "He won't come, he's drunk, he'll forget the apartment number. And if he does come, he'll never leave. Let me know if he's at the door, and I'll go in the bedroom and leave you two alone."

I waited—nothing. I was shocked by Claudio Brito's defeat. I gave up waiting and changed out of my dress.

Then someone rang the bell. Through the closed door I asked who it was. He said: "Claudio." I said: "Wait there on the bench in the hallway, I'll open the door in a minute." I put my dress back on. He had been a good poet, Claudio. What had he been doing with himself all this time?

He came in and soon was playing with my dog, saying that only animals understood him. I asked him if he would like some coffee. He said: "I only drink hard stuff, I've been drinking now for three days." I lied: I told him that unfortunately I didn't have any liquor in the house. And I again urged some coffee on him. He looked at me seriously and said:

"Don't give me orders . . ."

I answered:

"I'm not ordering you, I'm asking you to have some

coffee, I've got a thermos full of good coffee in the pantry."

He said that he liked his coffee strong. I brought him a teacup full of coffee with only a little sugar.

He didn't touch it. I insisted. Then he drank the coffee, while talking to my dog:

"If you break this cup you'll get it from me. See how he's looking at me, he understands me."

"I also understand you."

"You? The only thing that matters to you is literature."

"Well you're wrong. My children, family, friends, they come first."

He looked at me suspiciously, askance. And asked:

"Do you swear that literature doesn't matter?"

"I swear it," I answered with the assurance that comes from a sense of inner truth. And I added: "Any cat, any dog, is worth more than literature."

"In that case," he said, very moved, "shake my hand. I believe in you."

"Are you married?"

"A thousand times, I can't even remember anymore."

"Do you have children?"

"I have a five-year-old boy."

"I'll get you some more coffee."

I brought him back his cup almost full. He sipped at it. He said:

"You are a strange woman."

"No I'm not," I answered. "I'm very simple, there's nothing complicated about me."

He told me a story involving a certain Francisco, I didn't really understand who he was. I asked him:

"What kind of work do you do?"

"I don't work. I've retired as an alcoholic and mental case."

"You're no mental case at all. You just drink more than you should."

He told me that he had fought in Vietnam. And that he had been a seaman for two years. That he got along very well with the sea. And his eyes filled with tears. I said:

"Be a man and cry, cry as much as you like; be brave enough to cry. You must have plenty of reasons for crying."

"And here I am, drinking coffee and crying . . ."

"It doesn't matter, cry and make believe that I don't exist."

He cried a bit. He was a beautiful man, in need of a shave and thoroughly defeated. You could see that he had failed. Like all of us. He asked me if he could read me a poem. I said that I'd like to hear it. He opened a bag, took out a thick notebook, and laughed aloud while opening it.

Then he read the poem. It was simply beautiful. He had mixed dirty words with the greatest delicacies. "Oh Claudio," I wanted to cry out, "we are all failures, we will all die one day! Who, but *who* can say with sincerity that he has realized himself in this life? Success is a lie."

I said:

"It's so beautiful, that poem. Do you have others?"

"I have one other, but I must be bothering you. I'm sure you're wishing I'd go away."

"I don't want you to leave right now. I'll let you know when the time comes for you to leave. I go to bed early."

He looked for the poem in his notebook, didn't find it, gave up. He said:

"I know a little about you. I've even met your ex-husband."

I remained silent.

"You are beautiful."

I remained silent.

I was very sad. And didn't know what to do to help him. It's a terrible impotence not knowing how to help.

He said to me:

"If I kill myself some day . . ."

"You're not going to kill yourself, at all," I interrupted. "It's our duty to live. And to live can be good. Believe me."

It was I who was almost crying.

There was nothing I could do.

I asked him where he lived. He answered that he had a tiny apartment in Botafogo. I said: "Go home and sleep."

"First I have to see my son, he's got a fever."

"What's your son's name?"

He told me. I replied: "I have a son with the same name."

"I know."

"I'll give you a book of children's stories I once wrote for my children. Read it aloud to him."

I gave him the book and inscribed it. He put the book in what served as his carrying case. And I, despairing.

"Do you want a Coca-Cola?"

"You have a mania for offering people coffee and Coca-Cola."

"It's because I don't have anything else to offer."

At the door he kissed my hand. I walked him to the elevator, pressed the ground-floor button, and said to him: "Go with God, may God be with you."

The elevator went down. I went back to my apartment, turned off the lights, told my friend, who a moment later left herself, changed out of my dress, took some sleeping pills—and sat down in the living room to smoke a cigarette. I remembered that Claudio, a few minutes before, had asked for the cigarette which I had been smoking. I had given it to him. He had smoked it. He also had said: "Some day I'll kill someone."

"That's not true, I don't believe it."

He also told me how he had shot a dog that was suffering. I asked him if he had seen a film with the English title *They Shoot Horses, Don't They?* which had been called *The Night of the Desperate* in Portuguese. Yes, he had seen it.

I continued to smoke. My dog looked at me from the darkness.

That was yesterday, Saturday. Today is Sunday, the twelfth of May, Mother's Day. How can I be a mother to this man? I ask myself, and there is no answer.

There is no answer to anything.

I went to bed. I had died.

HE SOAKED ME UP

It did! It really happened!

Serjoca was a beautician. But he wanted nothing from women. He liked men.

And he did Aurelia Nascimento's make-up. Aurelia was pretty, and made up she became radiant. She was blonde, wore a wig and false eyelashes. They became friends. They went out together, you know, for a meal at a bar, that kind of thing.

Whenever Aurelia wanted to look good, she called up Serjoca. Serjoca himself was good-looking. He was tall and slender.

And so it went. A telephone call and they would agree to meet. She would dress well, outdoing herself. She wore contact lenses. And falsies. Her own breasts were pointed, pretty. She only used falsies because she was small breasted. Her mouth was a red rosebud. Her teeth were large and white.

One day, at six in the evening, just when the traffic was at its worst, Aurelia and Serjoca were standing in front of the Copacabana Palace waiting in vain for a taxi: Serjoca, worn out, was leaning against a tree. Aurelia was impatient. She suggested that they give the doorman ten cruzeiros to get them a cab. Serjoca refused: he was tough when it came to money.

It was almost seven o'clock. It was getting dark. What should they do?

Near them stood Affonso Carvalho. Manufacturer. Industrialist. He was waiting for his chauffeur with the Mercedes. It was hot out, but the car was air conditioned and had a telephone and refrigerator. Affonso had turned forty the day before.

He noticed the impatience of Aurelia, who was tapping her foot on the pavement. An interesting woman, thought Affonso. And she needs a ride. He turned to her:

"Excuse me, are you having some difficulty in finding a taxi?"

"I've been here since six o'clock and not one taxi has stopped for us. I can't take it much longer."

"My chauffeur will be here shortly," said Affonso. "Could I give you two a ride somewhere?"

"I would be most grateful, especially since my feet ache."

But she didn't say that she had corns. She hid the defect. She was fully made up and looked at the man with desire. Serjoca was very quiet.

Finally the chauffeur arrived, got out, and opened the door. The three got in. She in front, next to the chauffeur, the other two in back. She discreetly took off a shoe and sighed with relief.

"Where do you want to go?"

"We don't have anywhere in particular to go," Aurelia said, more and more aroused by Affonso's virile face.

He said: "What if we go to the Number One for a drink?"

"I'd love to," said Aurelia. "Wouldn't you, Serjoca?"

"Sure, I need a strong drink."

So they went to the bar, almost empty at that hour. And they talked. Affonso talked of metallurgy. The other two didn't understand a thing. But they pretended to understand. It was boring. But Affonso was carried away and, under the table, put his foot on top of Aurelia's foot. Precisely the foot with a corn. Excited, she responded. Then Affonso said:

"And what if we were to have dinner at my house? Today I'm having escargots and chicken with truffles. What do you say?"

"I'm starving."

Serjoca said nothing. He too was on fire for Affonso.

The apartment was carpeted in white, and there was a sculpture by Bruno Giorgi. They sat down, had another drink, and went into the dining room. A table of dark rosewood. A waiter serving from the left. Serjoca didn't know how to eat snails and fumbled ineptly with the special silverware. He didn't like it. But Aurelia enjoyed it a lot, even though she was afraid of smelling of garlic. And they all drank French champagne throughout the meal. No one wanted dessert, they just wanted coffee.

And they went into the living room. There Serjoca came alive. And began to talk as if he'd never stop. He threw languid glances at the businessman, who on his part was surprised at the eloquence of the good-looking young fellow. The next day he would call Aurelia to tell her Serjoca was a lovely person.

And they agreed to meet again. This time at a restaurant, the Albamar. They ate oysters to begin with. Again, Serjoca had trouble eating the oysters. I'm a failure, he thought.

But before they got together, Aurelia had called up Serjoca: she desperately needed to be made up. He went to her house.

Then, while she was being made up, she thought: Serjoca is taking off my face.

It felt as if he were wiping away her features: emptiness, a face merely of flesh. Brown flesh.

She felt ill. She excused herself and went to the bathroom to look at herself in the mirror. It was just as she had imagined: Serjoca had destroyed her face. Even the bones—and she had spectacular bone structure—even the bones had disappeared. He's soaking me up, she thought, he's going to destroy me. And it's on account of Affonso.

She returned dispirited. At the restaurant she scarcely spoke. Affonso spoke mostly with Serjoca, hardly looking at Aurelia: he was interested in the young man.

Finally, finally the luncheon ended.

Serjoca made a date to meet Affonso that night. Aurelia said she couldn't go, that she was tired. It was a lie: she wouldn't go because she didn't have a face to show.

Arriving home, she took a long bubble bath and sat thinking: a little longer and he'll take away my body as well. What could she do to recover what had been hers? Her individuality?

She left the bathroom thoughtfully. She dried herself with an enormous red towel. Thinking the whole time. She weighed herself on the scale: her weight was good. A little longer and he'll take away my weight as well, she thought.

She went to the mirror. She looked at herself for a long time. But she was nothing anymore.

Then—then, suddenly, she gave herself a hard slap on the left side of her face. To wake up. She stood still, looking at herself. And, as if it hadn't been enough, she gave herself two more slaps. To find herself.

And it really happened!

In the mirror she finally saw a human face. Sad. Delicate. She was Aurelia Nascimento. She had just been born. Nas-ci-men-to.

FOR THE TIME BEING

Since he had nothing to do, he went to pee. And then he reached ground zero.

To live involves such things: from time to time you hit rock bottom. And all this is for the time being. The time you live.

Today a girl called me, crying, saying that her father had died. That's how it is: neither more nor less.

One of my children is out of the country, the other came to have lunch with me. The meat was so tough you could hardly chew it. But we drank a chilled rosé. And we talked. I had asked him not to succumb to the impositions of a commercial world that exploited Mother's Day. He did what I asked: he gave me nothing. Or better, he gave me everything: his presence.

I worked all day long, now it's ten to six. The telephone doesn't ring. I'm alone. Alone in the world and in space. And when I telephone, the telephone rings and nobody answers. Or they say: he's sleeping.

The point is to know how to stand it. Because that's how things are. Sometimes you don't have anything to do and so you pee.

But if God made us so, then so be it. With empty hands. With nothing to talk about.

Friday night I went to a party, I didn't even know it was my friend's birthday, his wife hadn't told me.

There was quite a crowd. I noticed that a lot of people felt ill at ease.

What should I do? Call myself? There will be a sad busy signal, I know; once, absent-mindedly, I called my own number. How can I wake someone who is asleep? How can I call who I want to call? What can I do? Nothing: it's Sunday and even God rested then.

But now someone who was sleeping is already up and is coming to see me at eight o'clock. It is five after six.

We are in the midst of Indian summer: it's very hot. My fingers hurt from so much typing. You don't fool around with your fingertips. It's through the fingertips that we receive our fluids.

Should I have offered to go to the burial of the girl's father? Death would be too much for me today. Well, I know what I'll do: I'll eat. Then I'll come back. I go to the kitchen, my cook by chance isn't off today and will heat up some food for me. My cook is enormously fat: she weighs two hundred pounds. Two hundred pounds of insecurity, two hundred pounds of fear. I would like to kiss her smooth black face, but she wouldn't understand. I return to my typewriter while she heats up the food. I discover that I'm dying of hunger. I can hardly wait for her to call me.

Ah, I know what I'll do: I'll change my clothes. Then I'll eat, and then I'll return to the typewriter. So long.

I've already eaten. It was great. I drank a bit of rosé. Now I'll have some coffee. And turn on the air conditioning: in Brazil air conditioning isn't a luxury, it's a necessity. Especially for someone like me, who suffers a lot from the heat. It's six-thirty. I turn on my portable radio. To the Ministry of Education. But what sad music! You don't have to be sad to be well educated. I'll invite Chico Buarque, Tom Jobim, and Caetano Velloso over and ask each to bring his guitar. I want happiness, melancholy kills me little by little.

When you start to ask yourself: what for?—then things aren't going well. And I'm asking myself what for. But I know well enough that it's just "for the time being." It's twenty to seven. And for what is it twenty to seven?

Meanwhile I've made a phone call and, to my jubilation, it's already ten to seven. Never in my life have I said such a thing as "to my jubilation." It's really strange. Now and then I become half Machadian. Speaking of Machado de Assis, I miss him. It's hard to believe, but I don't have a single book of his on my shelf. José de Alencar, I don't even remember if I ever read him.

I'm full of yearning. Yearning for my children, yes, flesh of my flesh. Weak flesh, and I haven't read all the books. La chair est triste.

But you smoke and quickly feel better. It's five to seven. If I'm careless, I'll die. It's so simple. It's a question of a watch stopping. It's three minutes to seven. Should I or should I not turn on the TV? It's so boring watching television alone.

But finally I make up my mind and turn on the television. Sometimes one dies.

DAY BY DAY

Today is the thirteenth of May. The anniversary of the Freeing of the Slaves. Monday. Open market day. I turned on my portable radio, and they were playing the "Blue Danube." I was overjoyed. I got dressed, went downstairs, bought flowers in the name of him who died yesterday. Red and white carnations. As I have repeated to exhaustion, one day you die. And you die in red and white. The man who died was an innocent: he had worked for mankind, warning us that the world's food supply was coming to an end. There remains Laura, his wife. A strong woman, a clairvoyant woman, with black hair and black eyes. In a few days I'll pay her a visit. Or at least speak with her on the phone.

Yesterday, the twelfth of May, Mother's Day, the people who said they were coming didn't come. But I saw some friends, a couple, and we went out to eat together. Better that way. I don't want to depend on anyone else anymore. What I want is the "Blue Danube." Not the "Valse Triste" of Sibellius, if that's how one spells his name.

I went down again, going to Manuel's little shop to get new batteries for my radio. This is what I said to him:

"Do you remember the man who was playing the

43

harmonica Saturday? He used to be a great writer."

"Yes, I remember. It's sad. War trauma. He drinks all over the place."

I left.

When I got home someone called to tell me: think well before writing a pornographic book, ask yourself if it will add anything to your works. I answered:

"I've already asked my son's pardon, I told him not to read the book. I told him a bit about the stories I've written. He listened and said: that's o.k. I told him that my first story was called "Miss Algrave." He said: "grave" means tomb in English. Then I told him of the phone call from the girl who was crying because her father had died. My son said in consolation: he lived a full life. I said: he lived well.

But the person who called me got angry, I got angry, she hung up, I called her back, she didn't want to talk and hung up again.

If this book is published with "mala suerte" I'm lost. But one is lost in any case. There is no escape. We all suffer from war trauma.

I remembered something amusing. A friend of mine came one day to do her marketing right there in front of my house. But wearing shorts. And a stall keeper shouted at her:

"What thighs! What shape you're in!"

My friend got furious and said to him:

"Tell it to your mother!"

The man laughed, the creep.

Ah well. Who knows if this book will add anything to my works. Damn my works. I don't know why people attach so much importance to literature. And as for my name? To hell with it, I've got other things to think about.

I think, for example, of a friend who had a growth on her right breast and endured the fear alone until, almost on the eve of the operation, she told me. We were frightened. The forbidden word: cancer. I prayed a great deal. She prayed. And luckily it was benign, her husband called to tell me the news. The following day she called to say that it had been nothing but a "bag of water." I told her that next time she should arrange for a bag of fine leather, it would be more fun.

Having bought flowers and new batteries, I'm left without a penny in the house. But in a little while I'll call the drugstore, where they know me, and ask them to cash me a check for a hundred cruzeiros. Then it's off to the market.

But I'm a Sagittarius and a Scorpio, with Aquarius rising. And I'm vindictive. One day a couple invited me to Sunday dinner. And on Saturday afternoon, just like that, at the last moment, they told me that the dinner was off because they had to entertain a very important foreign visitor. Why didn't they invite me anyway? Why did they leave me alone on a Sunday? So I took my revenge. I'm not very nice. I no longer sought them out. And I won't accept their invitations anymore. So that's that.

I just remembered I have one hundred cruzeiros in a handbag. So I no longer have to call up the drugstore. I hate asking favors. I'm not going to call anyone. If someone wants to, they can come look for me. I'm going to play hard to get. From now on, no more fooling around.

In two weeks I'm going to Brasilia. To deliver a lecture. But—when they call me to set the exact time—I'm going to ask for something: that they don't make a fuss over me. That everything be done simply. I'll stay at a hotel because that way I feel free. The trouble is when I give a lecture I become so nervous that I read too fast and nobody understands. Once I went to Campos by air taxi and gave a lecture at the university there. Beforehand they had shown me some of my books in Braille. I didn't know what to say. And in the audience there were blind people. I was nervous. Afterward, there was a dinner in my honor. But I couldn't take it; I excused myself and went off to bed. In the morning they brought me something sweet called *chuvisco,* made from eggs and sugar. We were eating *chuviscos* at my house for quite a few days after that. I like to get a present. And to give one. It's good. Yolanda gave me some chocolates. Marly gave me a shopping bag that is very pretty. I gave Marly's daughter a little golden saint's medallion. The girl is bright and speaks French.

Now I'm going to tell a few stories about a girl named Nicole. Nicole said to her older brother, Marco: you look like a woman with all that long hair. Marco reacted with a violent kick because he's a real little man. Then Nicole quickly added:

"But don't worry about it, God is a woman!"

Then, softly, she whispered to her mother: I know that God is a man, but I don't want to get beaten up.

Nicole said to her cousin, who was horsing around at their grandmother's: don't behave like that, because once when I was like that grandma gave me such a slap I got knocked cold. When Nicole's mother heard of this, she reprimanded her. She then told Marco the story. Marco said:

"That's nothing. Once Adriana was fooling around at grandma's and I told her: better not because once when I was doing that grandma hit me so hard that I slept for a hundred years."

Didn't I say that today is a "Blue Danube" day? I am happy, in spite of the death of a good man, in spite of Claudio Brito, in spite of the phone call about my miserable literary work. I'll have another cup of coffee.

And a Coke. As Claudio Brito said, I've got a mania for Coca-Cola and coffee.

My dog is scratching his ear, and with such pleasure that he actually moans. I'm his mother.

I need some money. But how beautiful the "Blue Danube" is, it really is!

Long live the open market! Long live Claudio Brito! (I've changed the name, of course. Any similarity is merely coincidental.) Long live me! still alive!

And now I am done.

FOOTSTEPS

She was eighty-one years old. Her name was Dona Candida Raposo.

This woman was dizzy with life. Her dizziness increased when she went to spend a few days on a farm: the altitude, the green of the trees, the rain, all this made it worse. When she listened to Liszt she shivered from head to toe. She had been beautiful in her youth. And would become dizzy from deeply inhaling the smell of a rose.

Well, in the case of Dona Candida Raposo, the desire for pleasure didn't pass away.

Finally she had the great courage to go to a gynecologist. And she asked him, with her head bowed in shame:

"When will it pass?"

"When will what pass, my dear lady?"

"The thing."

"What thing?"

"The thing," she repeated. "The desire for pleasure," she finally said.

"My dear lady, I am sorry to say that it never goes away."

She looked at him in astonishment.

"But I'm eighty-one years old!"

"It doesn't matter, my dear. It's there till death."

"But it's hell!"

"That's life, Senhora Raposo."

So that's what life was then? This shamelessness?

"Then what should I do? Nobody wants me any-more . . ."

The doctor looked at her with compassion.

"There is no remedy, my dear lady."

"But what if I were to pay?"

"It wouldn't make any difference. You must remember that you are eighty-one years old."

"And . . . and what if I take care of it myself? Do you understand what I'm trying to say?"

"Yes," said the doctor. "It might help."

So she left the doctor's office. Her daughter was waiting for her down below with the car. Candida Raposo had lost her son in the war; he had been a young private. She had an intolerable pain in her heart: the pain of having survived a beloved one.

That very night she did what she could and, alone, satisfied herself. Silent fireworks. Afterward she cried. She was ashamed. From then on she used the same method. It was always sad. That's life, Senhora Raposo, that's life. Until the blessing of death.

Death.

She thought she heard the sound of footsteps. The footsteps of her husband, Antenor Raposo.

A COMPLICATED CASE

Well, then.

Whose father, with his tiepin, was the lover, the lover of the wife of the doctor who took care of his daughter, that is the daughter of the lover, and everyone knew all about it, and the wife of the doctor would hang a white towel in the window to signal the lover that he could come in, or else it was a colored towel and he couldn't come in.

But I'm getting all mixed up, or else it's the affair that is so involved, and I'll unravel it if I can. The realism here is invented. I beg your pardon, for besides recounting the facts I also guess, and what I guess I write down. I guess at reality. But this story isn't my baby. It belongs to people more able than I.

Well, the daughter had gangrene of the leg, and they had to amputate. This seventeen-year-old Jandira, more high-spirited than a young colt and with beautiful hair, was engaged to be married. The moment the fiancé saw the figure on crutches, all joyous, with a joy which he did not see was pathetic, well then, he had the courage simply to break off the engagement, without any remorse, since he didn't want to get stuck with a cripple. Everyone, including the poor mother of the girl, implored the fiancé to pretend that he still loved her, a thing which—they told him—wouldn't be so painful

since it would just be for a short while: that is, the
fiancée had just a short while to live.

And three months later—as if fulfilling a promise not
to weigh too heavily on the frail mind of her fiancé—
three months later she died, beautiful, with her beautiful hair, inconsolable, yearning for her fiancé, and
frightened of death as a child fears the dark: death is of
a great darkness. Or perhaps not. I don't know what it's
like, I haven't died yet, and even after dying I won't
know. Who knows, it might not be so dark. Death, I mean.

The fiancé, who was called by his family name, Bastos, lived, so it seems, even when his fiancée was alive,
he lived with a woman. And so he stayed on with her,
quite untroubled.

Well. One day that woman became jealous. And she
was very deliberate. I cannot omit cruel details. But
where was I, I've lost my place. Nothing to do but start
again, and on a new line and in a new paragraph, for
a better beginning.

Well. The woman was jealous, and while Bastos slept
she poured boiling water direct from the spout of the
tea kettle into his ear; he had just enough time to give
a bellow before passing out, a bellow which we can well
imagine was the worst scream that he had, the scream
of a beast. Bastos was taken to the hospital and remained between life and death, the one in furious com-
bat with the other.

The jealous virago got a little over a year in jail. From
which she came out to meet—can you guess who? Well,
to meet Bastos. At this stage, a Bastos much faded and,
of course, deaf forever, yes he, the very man who had
refused to forgive a physical defect.

What happened? Well, they moved in together again;
love is forever.

Meanwhile, the seventeen-year-old girl, long dead, nothing but vestiges remaining in her poor mother. And if I remember the young girl at an inopportune moment, it's due to the love I bear her.

Now it is that her father enters, like a man with nothing on his mind. He had continued to be the lover of the wife of the doctor who had treated his daughter so devotedly. The daughter, that is, of the lover. And everyone knew, the doctor and the mother of the dead ex-fiancée. I think that I've lost myself again, all this is a bit confusing, but what can I do?

The doctor, even knowing the young girl's father to be his wife's lover, had taken much care with the young bride-to-be, so very frightened by the darkness of which I spoke. The wife of the father—therefore the mother of the ex-bride-to-be—knew of the adulterous elegancies of her husband, who wore a gold watch, a jewel of a ring, and a diamond-studded tiepin. A well-to-do businessman, as one says, for people respect and praise at great length the rich and the victorious, right? He, the girl's father, dressed in a green suit with a pink striped shirt. How do I know? Look, I just know, the way one does with imaginative guessing. I know, and that's that.

I can't forget one detail. It's the following: the lover had a front tooth of gold, just for the luxury of it. And he smelled of garlic. All about him was the aura of pure garlic, and his lover didn't notice, she just wanted to have a lover, with or without the smell of food. How do I know? I just know.

I don't know to what end those people came, I've heard no further news. Did they separate? For it's an old story, and perhaps there have even been deaths among them, those people.

I'll add one important fact which, I don't know why,

explains the cursed origin of the whole story: it all happened in Niterói, with its waterfront planks always damp and grimy, and its ferry boats. Niterói is a mysterious place, and it has old, blackened houses. And could boiling water in a lover's ear happen there? I don't know.

What to make of this story? That, too, I don't know, I'm giving it as a present to whoever wants it, because I'm sick of it. And how! Sometimes people make me sick. Then it passes, and I become all curious and observant once again.

That's all.

PLAZA MAUÁ

The cabaret on Plaza Mauá was called The Erotica. And Luisa's stage name was Carla.

Carla was a dancer at The Erotica. She was married to Joaquim, who was killing himself working as a carpenter. And Carla "worked" at two jobs: dancing half nude and cheating on her husband.

Carla was beautiful. She had little teeth and a tiny waist. She was delicate throughout. She had scarcely any breasts, but she had well-shaped hips. She took an hour to make herself up: afterward, she seemed a porcelain doll. She was thirty but looked much younger.

There were no children. Joaquim and she couldn't get together. He worked until ten at night. She began work at exactly ten. She slept all day long.

Carla was a lazy Luisa. Arriving at night, when the time came to present herself to the public, she would begin to yawn, wishing she were in her nightgown in bed. This was also due to shyness. Incredible as it might seem, Carla was a timid Luisa. She stripped, yes, but the first moments of the dance, of voluptuous motion, were moments of shame. She only "warmed up" a few minutes later. Then she unfolded, she undulated, she gave all of herself. She was best at the samba. But a nice, romantic blues also turned her on.

She was asked to drink with the clients. She received

a commission per bottle. She always chose the most expensive drinks. And she pretended to drink: but hers wasn't alcohol. The idea was to get the clients drunk and make them spend. It was boring talking with them. They would caress her, passing their hands over her tiny breasts. And she in a scintillating bikini. Beautiful.

Once in a while she would sleep with a client. She would take the money, keep it well hidden in her bra, and the next day she would buy some new clothes. She had clothes without end. She bought blue jeans. And necklaces. A pile of necklaces. And bracelets, and rings.

Sometimes, just for variety's sake, she danced in blue jeans and without a bra, her breasts swinging among the flashing necklaces. She wore bangs and, using a black pencil, painted on a beauty mark close to her delicate lips. It was adorable. She wore long pendant earrings, sometimes pearl, sometimes imitation gold.

In moments of unhappiness, she turned to Celsinho, a man who wasn't a man. They understood each other well. She told him her troubles, complained about Joaquim, complained about inflation. Celsinho, a successful transvestite, listened to it all and gave her advice. They weren't rivals. They each worked their own turf.

Celsinho came from the nobility. He had given up everything to follow his vocation. He didn't dance. But he did wear lipstick and false eyelashes. The sailors of Plaza Mauá loved him. And he played hard to get. He only gave in at the very end. And he was paid in dollars. After changing the money on the black market, he invested it in the Banco Halles. He was very afraid of growing old, destitute and forsaken. Especially since an old transvestite is a sad thing. He took two envelopes of powdered proteins a day for energy. He had large hips and, from taking so many hormones, he had acquired a facsimile of breasts. Celsinho's stage name was Moleirão.

Moleirão and Carla brought good money to the owner of The Erotica. The smoke-filled atmosphere, the smell of alcohol. And the dance floor. It was tough being forced to dance with a drunken sailor. But what could you do. Everyone has his *métier*.

Celsinho had adopted a little girl of four. He was a real mother to her. He slept very little in order to look after the girl. And she lacked for nothing: she had only the best. Even a Portuguese nanny. On Sundays Celsinho took little Clareta to the zoo at the Quinta de Boa Vista. And they both ate popcorn. And they fed the monkeys. Little Clareta was afraid of the elephants. She asked: "Why do they have such big noses?"

Celsinho then told her a fantastic tale involving good fairies and bad fairies. Or else he would take her to the circus. And they would suck hard, clicking candies, the two of them. Celsinho wanted a brilliant future for little Clareta: marriage with a man of fortune, children, jewels.

Carla had a Siamese cat who looked at her with hard blue eyes. But Carla scarcely had time to take care of the creature: either she was sleeping, or dancing, or out shopping. The cat was named Leléu. And it drank milk with its delicate little red tongue.

Joaquim hardly saw Luisa. He refused to call her Carla. Joaquim was fat and short, of Italian descent. It had been a Portuguese woman neighbor who had given him the name Joaquim. His name was Joaquim Fioriti. Fioriti? There was nothing flowerlike about him.

The maid who worked for Joaquim and Luisa was a wily black woman who stole whatever she could. Luisa hardly ate, in order to keep her figure. Joaquim drowned himself in minestrone. The maid knew about everything, but kept her trap shut. It was her job to polish Carla's jewelry with Brasso and Silvo. When Joaquim was sleeping and Carla working, this maid, by the name of Silvinha, wore her mistress's jewelry. And she was kind of grayish-black in color.

This is how what happened happened.

Carla was confiding in Moleirão when she was asked to dance by a tall man with broad shoulders. Celsinho lusted after him. And he ate his heart out in envy. He was vindictive.

When the dance ended and Carla returned to sit down next to Moleirão, he could hardly hold in his rage. And Carla, innocent. It wasn't her fault she was attractive. And, in fact, the big man appealed to her. She said to Celsinho:

"I'd go to bed with that one for free."

Celsinho said nothing. It was almost three in the morning. The Erotica was full of men and women. Many mothers and housewives went there for the fun of it and to earn a bit of pocket money.

Then Carla said:

"It's so good to dance with a real man."

Celsinho sprang:

"But you're not a real woman!"

"Me? How come I'm not?" said the startled girl, who, dressed that night in black, in a long dress with long sleeves, looked like a nun. She did this on purpose to excite those men who desired a pure woman.

"You," screamed Celsinho, "are no woman at all! You don't even know how to fry an egg! And I do! I do! I do!"

Carla turned into Luisa. White, bewildered. She had been struck in her most intimate femininity. Confused, staring at Celsinho who had the face of a witch.

Carla didn't say a word. She stood up, crushed her cigarette in the ashtray, and, without turning to anyone, abandoning the party at its height, she left.

On foot, in black, on the Plaza Mauá at three in the morning. Like the lowest of whores. Alone. Without recourse. It was true: she didn't know how to fry an egg. And Celsinho was more of a woman than she.

The plaza was dark. And Luisa breathed deeply. She looked at the lampposts. The plaza was empty.

And in the sky, the stars.

PIG LATIN

Maria Aparecida—Cidinha, as they called her at home—was an English teacher. Neither rich nor poor: just properly comfortable. But she dressed to perfection. She looked wealthy. Even her suitcases were of high quality.

She lived in Minas Gerais and was going by train to Rio, where she would spend three days, and then take a plane to New York.

She was much sought after as a teacher. She loved perfection and was friendly, though strict. She wanted to perfect her English in the United States.

She took the seven o'clock train to Rio. It was really cold. And she with her suede coat and three suitcases. The car was empty, just an old woman sleeping in a corner under her shawl.

At the next station two men got on and sat down in the seat in front of Cidinha's. The train began to move. One man was tall, thin, with a little mustache and a cold eye, the other was short, paunchy, and bald. They looked at Cidinha. She quickly turned her eyes away and looked out the window.

It was uncomfortable in the coach. As if it were too hot. The girl uneasy. The men on the alert. My God, thought the girl, what could they want from me? There was no answer. And on top of it all she was a virgin. But why, oh why, had she thought of her own virginity?

The two men began to talk to each other. At first Cidinha didn't understand a word. It seemed a game. They spoke very quickly. But the language seemed vaguely familiar to her. What language was it?

Suddenly she understood: they were speaking Pig Latin—to perfection. Like this:

"Idday ouyay eckchay touay atthay ettypray ickchay?"

"Iay uresay idday. Eshay's ay eautybay. Eshay's inay ethay agbay."

In other words: "Did you check out that pretty chick? I sure did. She's a beauty. She's in the bag."

Cidinha pretended not to understand: to understand would be dangerous for her. The language was the same one they had used as children to protect themselves from the grownups. The two went on:

"Iay antway otay crewsay atthay irlgay. Atwhay outabay ouyay?"

"Emay ootay. Enwhay eway etgay otay ethay unneltay."

In other words they were going to rape her in the tunnel . . . What could she do? Cidinha didn't know, and she trembled with fear. She hardly knew herself. At least she had never known herself deep down. As for knowing the others, that made it even worse. Help me, Virgin Mary! Help me, help me!

"Fiay eshay esistsray eway ancay illkay erhay."

If she tried to resist they might kill her. So that's how it was.

"Eway ancay abstay erhay. Danay obray erhay."

Stab her to death! And rob her!

How could she tell them that she wasn't rich? That she was fragile, that the merest touch would kill her.

She got a cigarette out of her pocketbook in order to smoke and calm herself down. It didn't do any good. When would the next tunnel come? She had to think quickly, quickly, quickly.

Then the idea came to her: if I pretend that I am a prostitute, they'll give up, they wouldn't want a whore.

So she pulled up her skirt, made sensual movements—she didn't even know she knew how, so unknown was she to herself—and opened the top buttons on her blouse, leaving her breasts half exposed. The men suddenly in shock.

"Eshay's razycay."

In other words, "she's crazy."

And she undulated like no samba-dancer, down from the hills. She took her lipstick out of her bag and lavishly painted her lips. And she began to sing, off-key.

So the men began to laugh at her. They found Cidinha's foolishness amusing. She was desperate. And the tunnel?

The conductor appeared. He saw it all. He didn't say a thing. But he went and told the engineer. The engineer said:

"Let's do something about it. I'll turn her over to the police at the next station."

And the next station came.

The engineer climbed down, spoke with a soldier named José Lindalvo. José Lindalvo didn't fool around. He climbed into the car, saw Cidinha, grabbed her brutally by the arm, gathered up the three suitcases as best he could, and they both got off.

The two men burst out laughing.

In the small station painted blue and pink there was a young lady with a suitcase. She looked at Cidinha with scorn. She mounted the train, and it left.

Cidinha didn't know what to say to the police. How could she explain Pig Latin? She was taken to jail and booked. They called her the worst names. And she stayed locked up for three days. They let her smoke. She smoked like mad, inhaling, crushing the cigarettes on the cement floor. There was a fat cockroach crawling along the floor.

Finally they let her go. She took the next train to Rio. She had washed her face, she wasn't a prostitute anymore. What was bothering her was the following: when the two had spoken of raping her, she had wanted to be raped. She was shameless. Danay Iay maay aay orewhay. That was what she had discovered. Humiliation.

She arrived in Rio exhausted. She went to an inexpensive hotel. She quickly realized that she had missed her plane. At the airport she bought a new ticket.

And she walked through the streets of Copacabana, desolate she, desolate Copacabana.

It was on the corner of Rua Figueiredo Magalhães that she saw a newsstand. And hanging there the newspaper *O Día*. She couldn't have said why she bought it.

In black headlines were the words: "Girl Raped and Killed in Train."

She trembled all over. It had happened, then. And to the girl who had despised her.

She began to cry there in the street. She threw away the damned newspaper. She didn't want to know the details. She thought:

"Atefay siay placableimay."

Fate is implacable.

BETTER THAN TO BURN

She was tall, strong, and hairy. Mother Clara had a dark stubble and deep black eyes.

She had entered the convent at the will of her family: they wished to see her sheltered in the bosom of God. She obeyed.

She fulfilled her obligations without complaint. She had many obligations. And then there were prayers. She prayed with fervor.

And she went to confession every day. Every day the white host that crumbled apart in one's mouth.

But she began to get tired of living only among women. Women, women, women. She chose a friend as a confidant. She told her that she couldn't stand it anymore. Her friend counseled her:

"Mortify the body."

So she began to sleep on cold flagstones. And whipped herself with a scourge. It was useless. She just caught terrible colds and got all covered with welts.

She confessed to the priest. He ordered her to continue to mortify herself. She continued.

But at the moment in which the priest touched her mouth to give her the host, she had to control herself in order not to bite his hand. He noticed this but said nothing. There was a silent pact between them. Both mortified themselves.

She could no longer look at the almost naked body of Christ.

Mother Clara was of Portuguese descent, and, in secret, she shaved her hairy legs. If they found out, poor her! She told the priest. He turned pale. He guessed that her legs were strong, well-shaped.

One day at mealtime she began to cry. She didn't tell anybody why. She herself didn't know why she was crying.

And from then on she lived a life of weeping. In spite of eating little, she got fat. She had dark shadows under her eyes. Her voice, when she sang in church, was that of a contralto.

Until finally she said to the priest in the confessional:

"I can't stand it any longer, I swear I can't stand it any longer."

He said meditatively:

"It is better not to marry. But it is better to marry than to burn."

She asked for an audience with her superior. Her superior reprimanded her severely. But Mother Clara was firm: she wanted to leave the convent, she wanted to find a man, she wanted to get married. Her superior asked her to wait one year. She answered that she couldn't, that it had to be now.

She packed what little she had and made her getaway. She went to live in a boarding house for young women.

Her black hair grew opulent. And she seemed all up in the air and dreamy. She paid for her room and board with the money her family sent her. The family didn't accept what she had done. But they couldn't let her die of hunger.

She made her own little dresses of cheap material on a sewing machine that a young girl at the boarding house lent her. Dresses with long sleeves, modestly cut, below the knees.

And nothing happened. She prayed a great deal that something good would come to her. In the form of a man.

And it really did.

She went to a snack bar to buy a bottle of mineral water. The owner was a dapper Portuguese who became enchanted by Clara's discreet manners. He didn't want her to pay for the mineral water. She blushed.

But she came back the next day to buy some coconut sweets. Again she didn't pay. The Portuguese, Antonio by name, called forth his courage and invited her to the movies. She refused.

The next day she returned to have a cup of coffee. Antonio promised her that he wouldn't touch her if they went to the movies together. She accepted.

They went to see a movie, but they didn't pay any attention to it. At the end of the movie they were holding hands.

Soon they were meeting for long walks. She with her black hair. He in a suit and tie.

Then one night he said to her:

"I'm rich, the snack bar earns enough for us to get married. Do you want to?"

"I want to," she answered gravely.

They were married in church and also had a civil ceremony. At church, the priest who united them was the one who had told her it was better to marry than to burn. They went to spend their feverish honeymoon in Lisbon. Antonio left his snack bar in the care of his brother.

She came back pregnant, satisfied, happy.

They had four children, all of them boys, all of them hairy.

BUT IT'S GOING TO RAIN

Maria Angelica de Andrade had sixty years to her credit. And a lover, Alexander, aged nineteen.

Everyone knew that the boy was taking advantage of Maria Angelica. Only Maria Angelica didn't suspect a thing.

This is how it began: Alexander was a delivery boy for a pharmacy, and he rang the doorbell at Maria Angelica's house. She herself opened the door. And discovered a young man, tall, strong, very beautiful. Instead of taking the medicine she had ordered and paying for it, she asked him, rather shocked at her own daring, if he wouldn't like to come in for a cup of coffee.

Alexander was surprised and said no thank you. But she insisted. She added that there was some cake as well.

The young fellow hesitated, clearly ill at ease. But he said:

"If it's just for a minute, I can come in, then I have to go back to work."

He entered. Maria Angelica didn't know that she was already in love. She gave him a thick slice of cake and coffee with milk. While he ate rather uneasily, she gazed dotingly at him. He was strength, youth, and sex, left behind so long ago. The youngster finished eating and drinking, and wiped his mouth on his sleeve. Maria Angelica didn't find this bad manners: she was delighted, she found him natural, simple, enchanting.

"Now I'd better get going, my boss will really let me have it if I'm late."

She was captivated. She noticed that he had a few pimples on his face. But that didn't detract from his beauty and his masculinity: his hormones were bubbling away. That, indeed, was a man! She gave him an enormous tip, quite out of proportion, which surprised the young man. And she said in a small singing voice and with the affectations of a romantic little girl:

"I will only let you go if you promise to come back! Today! Because I am going to order some vitamins from the pharmacy . . ."

An hour later he was back with the vitamins. She had changed her clothes and was now wearing a dressing gown of transparent lace. One could see the brand name on her underpants. She asked him to come in. She told him that she was a widow. It was her way of informing him that she was available. But the young man didn't understand.

She invited him through her nicely decorated apartment, leaving him agape. She took him to her bedroom. She didn't know how to get him to understand. Finally she said to him:

"Let me give you a little kiss!"

Startled, the boy held out his face. But she got to his mouth fast enough and practically devoured him.

"Ma'am," said the nervous boy, "please control yourself! Are you feeling all right?"

"I can't control myself! I love you! Come to bed with me!"

"Are you crazy?!"

"No, I'm not crazy! Or rather yes, I'm crazy about you!" she cried out as she pulled back the purple bedspread from the large double bed.

And seeing that he would never understand, she said to him, dying of shame:

"Come to bed with me . . ."

"Me?!"

"I'll give you a great big present! I'll give you a car!"

A car? The boy's eyes glistened with desire. A car! It was all that he wanted in life. Distrustfully he asked:

"A Karmann-Ghia?"

"Yes, my love, whatever you desire!"

What happened next was horrible. You needn't know. Maria Angelica—O Lord, have mercy on me, forgive me for having to write this—Maria Angelica gave little screams as they made love. And Alexander, having to endure it with nausea, with loathing. It left him rankling for the rest of his life. He felt that he would never again be able to sleep with a woman. Which, in fact, is what eventually happened: by the age of twenty-seven he was impotent.

And they became lovers. He didn't live with her on account of the neighbors. He wanted to live in a luxury hotel: he took breakfast in bed. Soon after, he quit his job. He bought the most expensive shirts. He went to a dermatologist, and the pimples disappeared.

Maria Angelica could hardly believe her luck. What did she care about the maids who almost laughed in her face.

One of her friends warned her:

"Maria Angelica, don't you see that the kid is a scoundrel? That he is taking advantage of you?"

"I won't allow you to call Alex a scoundrel! He loves me!"

One day Alex showed his true mettle. He said to her:

"I'm going to spend a couple of days away from Rio with a girl I know. I need some money."

They were terrible days for Maria Angelica. She

didn't leave the house, she didn't take a bath, she scarcely ate. It was only due to stubbornness that she still believed in God. For God had abandoned her. She was forced to be painfully herself.

Five days later he returned, all dandified, all happiness. He brought her a present of a can of chunky guava jam. She ate some and broke a tooth. She had to go to the dentist to have a false tooth put in.

And so life went on. The bills increased. Alexander exigent. Maria Angelica worried. On her sixty-first birthday he didn't appear. She sat alone in front of the birthday cake.

Then—then it happened.

Alexander said to her:

"I need a million cruzeiros."

"A million?" gasped Maria Angelica.

"Yes," he answered, irritated, "a billion old style!"

"But . . . but I don't have that much money . . ."

"Sell the apartment, then, and sell your Mercedes, get rid of the chauffeur."

"Even then it wouldn't be enough, my darling, have pity on me!"

The young man became furious:

"You disgusting old pig! You bitch! Without that billion I won't show up again for your disgusting orgies."

And, in a burst of hatred, he left, slamming the door behind him.

Maria Angelica just stood there. Her whole body ached.

Then she slowly went to sit down on the sofa in the living room. She looked like someone wounded in battle. But there was no Red Cross to help her. She was quiet, motionless. Without a word to say.

It looks, she thought, it looks as if it's going to rain.

WHERE YOU WERE
AT NIGHT

IN SEARCH OF DIGNITY

Senhora Jorge B. Xavier simply couldn't have said how she had gotten there. Not through some main gate. It seemed to her that, half in a dream, she had entered through a kind of narrow opening in the midst of the rubble of a building under construction, as if she had slipped sideways through a hole made just for her. The fact is, the first she knew, she was already inside.

Yes, the first she knew, she realized that she was very much inside. She was walking endlessly through the subterranean passages of Maracanã Stadium, or at least through what seemed to be narrow vaults leading to closed rooms which, when one entered, revealed but a single window giving out onto the stadium. The stadium, at that hour torridly deserted, shimmered beneath the glaring sun with an unusual heat, there on that midwinter day.

Then the lady went down a dark passage. It led her to another, even darker, one. It seemed to her that the ceilings of the passages were low.

And then this passage led her to another, which, in its turn, led her to another.

She rounded a bend in the deserted passage. And then she came to another bend. Which led her to another passage which led to another bend.

And so she continued automatically to follow passages that always led into other passages. Where would the room for the inaugural lecture be? For it was just outside that room that she would be meeting the people whom she had planned to meet. It was possible that the lecture had already begun. She would miss it, she who made an effort to miss nothing *cultural,* for that way she kept herself young within, though for that matter even externally no one guessed that she was almost seventy—everyone took her for fifty-seven.

But now, lost in the dark inner meanderings of Maracanã, the lady was dragging the leaden feet of age.

It was then that she suddenly met a man in the passageway, sprung up from nowhere, and asked him about the lecture, which he claimed to know nothing about. But this man asked a second man, who also suddenly turned up at a bend in the passage.

Then this second man informed them that, close to the righthand stands, he had seen, right out in the open "two ladies and a gentleman, one of the ladies dressed in red." Senhora Xavier had her doubts as to whether those people were the group she was supposed to meet before the lecture; in fact, by now she had lost sight of the reason why she was walking on and on without ever stopping. Nonetheless, she followed the man to the stadium, where she stopped, dazzled, in the hollow space of wide-open light and gaping stillness, the naked stadium disemboweled, with neither game nor players. Above all, without a crowd. There was a crowd, though, dwelling in the emptiness of its utter absence.

The two ladies and the gentleman, had they already disappeared down some passageway?

Then the man said in an unexpectedly defiant tone: "Well, I'll look for them for you, and one way or another I'll find those people, they couldn't have disappeared into thin air."

And, in fact, far in the distance, they both saw them. But a second later they disappeared again. It seemed a childish game in which Senhora Jorge B. Xavier was mocked by muffled bursts of laughter.

And so she went on with the man through other passages. And then that man himself, going round a corner, disappeared.

The lady had by then given up on the lecture, which, in truth, didn't really matter much to her. Just so long as she got out of that tangle of endless paths. Was there no way out? Now she felt as if she were in an elevator stuck between two floors. Was there no way out?

Then it was that she suddenly remembered her friend's instructions over the phone: "it's not far from Maracanã Stadium." In the face of this memory, she understood her error, that of a befuddled, distracted person who only hears half of what is said, the rest remaining submerged. Senhora Xavier was very inattentive. Well then, so the appointment wasn't at Maracanã, it was just nearby. Nonetheless, her little destiny had willed her lost in the labyrinth.

Well then, now the struggle became even more intense: she wanted desperately to get out, but didn't know how, nor where to turn. And once again there appeared in the passageway that man who had been looking for the others, and once again he promised he would find them since they couldn't have disappeared into thin air. That's exactly what he said:

"Those people couldn't have disappeared into thin air!"

The lady replied:

"You needn't take the trouble to search any longer, thank you. Thank you so much. The place where I have to meet the others isn't in Maracanã."

The man stopped dead in his tracks and looked at her in astonishment:

"But what are you doing here then, Ma'am?"

She wanted to explain that that's what her life was like, but not knowing what she meant by "that's what it's like" or "her life" she didn't answer. The man, now wary, somewhat suspicious, persisted in his questioning: what was she doing there? Nothing, answered the lady, but just in her mind, for by then she was on the point of collapsing from exhaustion. So she didn't answer him; she let him think she was crazy. In any case, she never explained herself. She knew that the man considered her crazy—and who could say she was not? For didn't she feel that thing she called "that" out of shame? Though she knew her so-called mental health was so good it could only be compared to her physical health. A physical health now broken, for her feet were dragging from years of walking through that labyrinth. Her way of the cross. Dressed in thick wool, she was suffocating, drenched with sweat in that unexpected heat of the height of summer, that summer day that was a freak of winter. Her legs ached, ached from the weight of the old cross. She had already, in some way, resigned herself to never again leaving Maracanã, and to dying there of a worn-out heart.

Then, as always, it was only after you had given up on what you wanted that it happened. What suddenly came to her was an idea: "but what an old nut I am." Why not, instead of continuing to ask after the people who weren't there, why not look for the man and ask him how to get out of the passageways? For what she really wanted was just to get out and not to meet anyone at all.

She finally found the man as she turned a corner.

And she spoke to him in a voice a bit tremulous and hoarse with exhaustion and the fear of hoping in vain. The suspicious man agreed more than readily that indeed it would be better for her to go home and said to her with great care: "You don't seem, Ma'am, to be quite right in your head, perhaps it's this strange heat."

Having said this, the man, quite simply, entered the first passageway with her and, turning a bend, they came upon the two large gates, wide open. Just like that? As easy as that?

Just like that.

Then it occurred to the lady, though she drew no conclusions, that it was only for her that it had become impossible to find the exit. Senhora Xavier was only a bit bewildered, for at the same time she was used to it. In truth, everyone has their own path to follow endlessly, that is part of our destiny, which she wasn't sure whether she believed in or not.

And there was a taxi going by. She signaled it to stop and said to the driver, controlling her voice, which was getting older and more tired by the moment:

"Young man, I'm not sure exactly of the address, I've forgotten. But I do know that the house is on a street—I-don't-remember-anymore-which-one, but it has something to do with 'Gusmão' and it crosses a street which, if I'm not mistaken, is called Colonel-something-or-other."

The driver was patient, as if with a child: "Well now, no need to panic, we'll just go along and calmly look for a street with Gusmão in the middle and a Colonel at the end," he said, turning around with a smile and a conspiratorial wink that seemed indecent. They took off with a jolt that shook her to the very innards.

Then, suddenly, she recognized the people she was

looking for, standing on the sidewalk in front of a large establishment. It was, however, as if the purpose were to arrive, not to hear the talk, which by then had been totally forgotten, for Senhora Xavier had lost sight of her goal. And she didn't know in the name of what she had been walking and walking so. Then she noticed that she was utterly exhausted, quite beyond her strength, and she wanted to leave; the lecture was a nightmare. So she asked a lady of some importance whom she vaguely knew, and who had a car and chauffeur, to take her home, as she wasn't feeling well in that strange heat. The chauffeur would only be returning in an hour. So Senhora Xavier sat down on a chair that was brought out into the hallway for her, there she sat, erect in her tight belt, cut off from the culture that was going on opposite her in the closed lecture hall. From which not a sound could be heard. Culture hardly mattered to her. And there she was in the labyrinth of sixty seconds and sixty minutes which would lead her to an hour.

Then the important lady came and said the following: that a car was at the door, but that she would like to inform her that since the chauffeur had called to say he would be quite late and since she hadn't been feeling well, she had stopped the first taxi she had seen. Why hadn't Senhora Xavier herself had the idea of calling a taxi, instead of allowing herself to submit to the wanderings of time as she waited? So Senhora Jorge B. Xavier thanked her with great politeness. She was always very polite and well bred. She got into the taxi and said:

"Leblon, if you please."

Her mind was empty, her brain felt starved.

After a while, she noticed that although they went on

and on they always ended up returning to the same square. Why couldn't they get out of there? Could it be that once again there was no way out? The driver finally confessed that he didn't know the South Side, that he just worked the North Side. And she didn't know how to direct him. The cross of her years weighed heavier and heavier, and the renewed absence of an exit merely brought back the black magic of the passageways of Maracanã. There was no way to free themselves of the square! Then the driver suggested she take another taxi, and he went so far as to signal one that was just alongside them. She thanked him most modestly, she was always formal with everyone, even with those she knew. Besides which she was very nice. In the new taxi she said with some trepidation:

"If it isn't too much trouble, could you take me to Leblon."

And, quite easily, they left the square behind and passed through new streets.

It was while unlocking her apartment door that she had the desire, just in her mind, in a fantasy, to whimper out loud. But she wasn't one to whine or complain. In passing, she told the maid that she didn't want any phone calls. She went straight to her room, took off all her clothes, swallowed a pill without water, and then waited for it to take effect.

Meanwhile, she smoked. She remembered that it was August, and they say that August brings bad luck. But September would arrive one day, like a way out. And September, for some reason, was the month of May: a lighter, more transparent month. She was vaguely thinking all this when drowsiness finally came and she fell asleep.

When she awoke hours later, she noticed that it was

raining a thin, icy rain; it was as cold as a knifeblade. Naked in her bed, she lay there freezing. Then she thought how strange it was, an old woman, naked. She remembered that she had planned to buy a woolen scarf. She looked at the clock: she would still find the shop open. She took a taxi and said:

"Ipanema, if you please."

The man said:

"What did you say? The Botanical Garden?"

"Ipanema, please," the lady said again, much surprised. It was the absurdity of a total misapprehension: for what did the words "Ipanema" and "Botanical Garden" have in common? But once again she thought vaguely that "that's what her life was like."

She quickly made her purchase and found herself on the already darkened street with nothing to do. For Senhor Jorge B. Xavier had gone to São Paulo the day before and would only return the following day.

So, back home again, between taking another sleeping pill or doing something else, she opted for the latter, for she remembered that now she could again search for that lost bill of exchange. From the little she understood, the paper represented money. For two days she had been searching the entire house with great care, even the kitchen, but in vain. Now it occurred to her: why not under the bed? Perhaps. So she knelt down on the floor. But she quickly felt tired supporting herself just on her knees, so she got down on her hands as well.

Then she noticed that she was on all fours.

She stayed like that for a while, maybe thinking, maybe not. Who knows, maybe Senhora Xavier was tired of being a human being. Now she was a bitch on all fours. Without the least nobility. Her last pride was gone. On all fours, a bit pensive, perhaps. But beneath the bed there was only dust.

She got up with a great effort of her worn-out joints and saw that there was nothing left to do but confront realistically—and it was with a painful effort that she saw reality—to confront realistically the fact that the letter was lost and that to continue to search for it would be to never escape from Maracanã.

And, as always, no sooner had she given up searching, than, opening the little handkerchief drawer in order to take one out—there was the bill of exchange.

So the lady, tired from the strain of having been on all fours, sat down on the bed and, just like that, began gently to cry. It seemed more like a rambling Arabic litany. For thirty years she hadn't cried, but now she was so tired. If that was really crying. No, it wasn't. It was something. Finally she blew her nose. Then she thought the following: that she would force "destiny" and would have a greater destiny. With will power everything is possible, she thought, without the least conviction. And this business of being bound by a destiny had occurred to her because she had already begun, without wishing to, to think about "that."

But then it happened that the lady also thought the following: it was too late to have a destiny. She felt she would gladly make any kind of exchange with another being. It was then that it occurred to her that there was no one with whom to exchange: that whatever she might be, she was she and couldn't transform herself into another unique being. Everyone was unique. Senhora Jorge B. Xavier was, too.

But everything that had happened to her so far was better than feeling "that." And it came, with its long passageways without end. "That," freed now of all shame, was the painful hunger of her entrails, the hunger to be possessed by television's unattainable idol. She never missed a single one of his shows. Well then, since she couldn't stop herself from thinking of him, the thing to do was to let herself think and remember once again the virginal-girlish face of Roberto Carlos, my love.

She went to wash her hands, dirty with dust, and saw herself in the bathroom mirror. Then Senhora Xavier thought: If I really wish it, but really really, he will be mine, for at least one night. She believed vaguely in the power of the will. Once again she let herself get entangled in a desire that was twisted and strangled.

But, who knows? If she were to give up on Roberto Carlos, then something might happen between them. Senhora Xavier pondered the subject a bit. Then cunningly she pretended to have given up on Roberto Carlos. But she knew full well that the magical surrender only gave positive results when it was real, and not merely a trick used to achieve an end. Reality demanded much of this lady. She looked at herself in the mirror to see if her face was turning bestial under the influence of her feelings. But it was a quiet face that had long ago ceased to show what she felt. In fact, her face had never shown anything but good breeding. And now it was nothing but the mask of a seventy-year-old woman. And then her face, lightly made-up, seemed to her that of a clown. The lady forced an unwilling smile to see if it improved matters. It did not.

On the outside—she saw in the mirror—she was something dried up, like a dry fig. But inside she wasn't baked through. On the contrary. Within, she felt like a moist gum, as soft as a toothless gum.

Then she searched for a thought that would spiritualize her or fry her to a frizzle once and for all. But she had never been spiritual. And because of Roberto Carlos, the lady was immersed in the darkness of matter, where she was profoundly anonymous.

Standing there in the bathroom, she was as anonymous as a hen.

In a fraction of a fleeting second, almost unconsciously, she glimpsed the truth that all people are anonymous. For no one is the other, and an other doesn't know the other. And so—so, a person is anonymous. And now she was engulfed in that deep and fatal well, the insurrection of the body. A body with its depths hidden, the darkness of the murky evil of her instincts, alive as lizards and rats. And everything out of joint, fruit out of season? Why hadn't the other old women ever warned her that until the very end this could happen? In old men, she had certainly seen lascivious stares. But in old women, never. Out of season. And she, alive as if she were still somebody, she who was nobody.

Senhora Jorge B. Xavier was nobody.

And then she wanted to have beautiful, romantic sentiments in response to the delicacy of Roberto Carlos' face. But she didn't succeed: his delicacy merely carried her to a dark passageway of sensuality. And lechery was her damnation. It was a lowly hunger: she wanted to eat Roberto Carlos' mouth. She wasn't romantic, she was coarse in matters of love. Right there in the bathroom, facing the mirror above the sink.

With her age indelibly maculate.

Without even a single sublime thought to serve her as a rudder and ennoble her existence.

Then she began to take down her hair, and slowly she began to comb it. It needed to be dyed again, the white roots were already showing. And then the lady thought the following: in my life there has never been a climax as in the stories one reads. The climax was Roberto Carlos. Pondering, she came to the conclusion that she would die secretly, just as she had lived secretly. But she also understood that all death is secret.

From the depths of her future death, she imagined seeing in the mirror the yearned-for image of Roberto Carlos, with that soft, curly hair he had. There she was, imprisoned by desire, out of season, just like that summer day in the middle of winter. Imprisoned in the mesh of the passageways of Maracanã. Imprisoned in the mortal secret of the old. Only she wasn't used to being almost seventy, she lacked practice, she hadn't the least experience.

Then she said out loud and all alone:

"Dearest Bobby Carlos, babe."

And even added: my love. She heard her voice with wonder, as if for the first time making, quite without any shame or sense of guilt, a confession which, nevertheless, ought to have been shameful. Musing, the lady imagined that possibly Bobby wouldn't accept her love, since she herself saw that this love was quite maudlin, stickily voluptuous and lecherous. And Roberto Carlos seemed so chaste, so asexual.

Her lips, lightly rouged, were they still kissable? Or might it be, perhaps, nauseating to kiss the mouth of an old woman? She examined her lips from close, and without expression. And still without expression, she softly sang the chorus of Roberto Carlos' most famous song: "In this winter cold, heat me good and well, and everything else, babe, can go to hell."

It was then that Senhora Jorge B. Xavier suddenly bent over the basin as if to vomit up her very guts and interrupted her life with a shattering silence: there must be a way o u t!

THE DEPARTURE OF THE TRAIN

The departure was from Central Station, with its enormous clock, the largest in the world. It showed the time as six in the morning. Angela Pralini paid for her taxi and picked up her small suitcase. Dona Maria Rita Alvarenga Chagas Souza Melo emerged from her daughter's Opala and set off toward the tracks. A well-dressed elderly lady with jewels. From the wrinkles that masked her came the pure form of a nose lost in age and of a mouth that once must have been full and sensitive. But what does it matter. You reach a certain point—and what once was, no longer matters. A new race begins. An old woman cannot make herself understood. She received a cold kiss from her daughter, who left before the train departed. She had first helped her up into the car. Since no middle seats were free, she had taken a place to one side. When the locomotive began to move, it surprised her a bit: she hadn't expected the train to go in that direction and had seated herself facing backward.

Angela Pralini noticed her startled movement and asked: "Would you like to change places with me?"

Dona Maria Rita, delicately surprised, said no, thank you, for her it was all the same. But she seemed troubled. She passed her hand over her cameo, with its gold filigree, pinned to her breast, fumbled at her broach, took her hand away, lifted it to her felt hat with its cloth rose, and again took it away. Stiff. Offended? Finally she asked Angela Pralini:

"Could it be for my sake you're offering to change seats?"

Surprised, Angela Pralini said no, and the old woman was surprised for the same reason: one doesn't accept favors from an old lady. She smiled a little too much, and her stretched lips covered with talcum powder split into dry furrows: she was enchanted. And a bit excited:

"How very nice of you," she said, "how very kind."

There was a moment of confusion as Angela Pralini also laughed, and the old woman continued to laugh, showing her spotless dentures. She gave a discreet little pull downward on her belt, which was too tight.

"How kind of you," she repeated.

She then composed herself again, rather suddenly, crossing her hands over her purse, which held everything you could imagine. Her wrinkles, when she laughed, had taken on meaning, thought Angela. Now they were once again incomprehensible, superimposed once again on a face unmalleable. But Angela had already broken her tranquillity. She had already seen many nervous young ladies telling themselves: if I laugh anymore I will ruin everything, it will be ridiculous, I have to stop—and it had been impossible. The situation was very sad. With great pity, Angela saw a cruel wart on her chin, a wart from which emerged a stiff black hair. But Angela had taken her peace away. You could see she was about to smile at any moment: Angela had the old woman on tenterhooks. Now she was one of those little old ladies who seem to think that they are always late, that the hour has passed. A moment later she couldn't contain herself and got up to look out the window, as if it were impossible to stay seated.

"Are you trying to close the window, ma'am," said a young fellow listening to Handel on a transistor radio.

"Ah," she exclaimed, terrified.

Oh, no, thought Angela, everything was getting spoiled, the young man shouldn't have said that, it was too much, no one should have touched her again. For the old woman, almost on the point of losing the attitude which had sustained her throughout life, almost about to lose a certain bitterness, quavered like harpsichord music between a smile and the deepest enchantment:

"No, no, no," she said with a false tone of authority, "not at all, thank you, I only wanted to look out."

She sat down immediately as if being observed by the politeness of the young man and the girl. The old woman, before getting into the train, had made the sign of the cross three times over her heart, discreetly kissing her fingertips. She was in a black dress with a genuine lace collar and a cameo of pure gold. On her dark left hand were a widow's two thick wedding rings, thick the way they don't make them anymore. From the next car you could hear a group of girl scouts singing their high-pitched praises of "Brazil." Luckily it was in the next car. The music on the young fellow's radio merged with the music of another fellow: he was listening to Edith Piaf singing "J'attendrai."

It was then that the train suddenly gave a jolt and the wheels began to move. The departure had begun. The old woman said softly: Ah, Jesus! She had soaked herself in sweet Jesus. Amen. A woman's transistor informed them that it was six-thirty in the morning, a chilly morning. The old woman thought: Brazil was improving its road signs. A certain Kissinger seemed to be running the world.

No one knows where I am, thought Angela Pralini, and this frightened her somewhat, she was a fugitive.

"My name is Maria Rita Alvarenga Chagas Souza Melo—Alvarenga Chagas was my father's surname," she added, as if begging pardon for having to say so many words just in telling her name. "Chagas," she added modestly, "were the Chagas, the 'stigmata,' of Christ. But you can call me Dona Maria Ritinha. And your name? What might one call you?"

"My name is Angela Pralini. I'm going to spend six months with my uncles on their farm. And you?"

"Ah, I'm going to my son's farm. I'm going to stay there for the rest of my life, my daughter took me to the train, and my son will pick me up with his cart at the station. I am like a package being passed from hand to hand."

Angela's uncles had no children and treated her like a daughter. Angela remembered the note she had left for Eduardo: "Don't look for me. I am vanishing from your life forever. I love you more than ever. Farewell. I would have been more yours had you wished it so."

They remained silent. Angela Pralini gave herself up to the rhythmic sound of the train. Dona Maria Rita looked again at that ring of diamonds and pearls on her finger and smoothed down her golden cameo: "I am old but I am rich, richer than anyone in this car. I am rich, I am rich." She glanced at her watch, but in order to see the thick gold plate rather than the time. "I am very rich, I am not just any old lady." But she knew, ah, how well she knew, that she was indeed any old lady, just a little old lady frightened of the littlest things. She remembered herself, the whole day all alone in the rocking chair, alone with the servants, while her "public relations" daughter spent the whole day out, only returning at eight in the evening, and not even giving her a kiss. She had gotten up this morning at five o'clock, everything still dark; and it had been cold.

After the kindness of the young man she had been extraordinarily excited, and all smiles. She looked drained. With her laugh she revealed herself as one of those little old ladies with a mouthful of teeth. The discordant cruelty of teeth. The young man had already moved off. She opened and shut her eyelids. Suddenly she tapped Angela on the thigh, quickly and gently:

"Today everyone is truly, but truly friendly. How really nice, how very nice!"

Angela smiled. The old woman continued to smile without taking her deep and empty eyes from those of the girl. "Come on, let's go, let's go," they snapped at her from all sides, and she looked here and there as if to choose. "Let's go, let's go." They jostled against her, laughing from all sides, and she fluttered, there, smiling, dainty, refined.

"How friendly everyone is on this train," she said.

Suddenly she tried to recompose herself, she cleared her throat unnecessarily, she drew herself in. It was going to be difficult. She feared that she had reached the point where she wouldn't be able to stop herself. She held herself severe and trembling, closing her lips over her innumerable teeth. But she couldn't fool anyone: her face had such hope in it that it disturbed the eyes of whoever looked at her. She no longer depended on anyone: now that they had touched her, she could go away—she, alone, tall, thin, radiant. She still would have liked to say something and in fact was preparing a sociable nod of the head, full of studied grace. Angela wondered if she would know how to express herself. She seemed to be thinking and thinking and then to find with tenderness a thought all ready-made in which somehow or other she could cradle her feelings. She said with the care and wisdom of the aged, as if it were necessary to put on such an air in order to speak like an elderly person:

"Youth! Gracious youth."

Her laughter was somewhat forced. "Was she going to have an attack of nerves?" thought Angela Pralini. For she was so marvelous. But now she cleared her throat again with austerity, tapping the seat with her fingertips as if urgently calling an orchestra to order for a new piece. She opened her purse, took out a small square of newspaper, unfolded it, unfolded it until it had become a large and normal newspaper from three days before—as Angela saw from the date. She began to read.

Angela had lost seven kilos. On the farm she would eat herself sick: bean stew and cabbage à la Mineira, to regain the precious lost kilos. She was this thin from having tried to keep up with Eduardo's brilliant, uninterrupted chain of thought: she had drunk coffee without sugar endlessly in order to stay awake. Angela Pralini had very pretty breasts, they were her strong point. She had pointed ears and a pretty, kissable, rounded mouth. Eyes with dark shadows. She took advantage of the scream of the train's whistle so that it might become her own scream. It was a sharp cry, hers, but turned inward. She was the woman who had drunk the most whiskey in Eduardo's group. She could take six or seven in a row, retaining a terrifying lucidity. At the farm she would drink thick cow's milk. One thing linked the old woman to Angela: both were going to be received with open arms, but neither knew this of the other. Angela suddenly shivered: who would give the dog its last day of deworming pills. Ah, Ulysses, she thought, to the dog, I didn't abandon you because I wanted to, it's that I had to flee Eduardo, before he destroyed me completely with his lucidity: a lucidity that illumined too much and singed everything. Angela knew that her uncles had a medicine for snakebite: she intended to enter the heart of the thick, verdant forest, with high boots smeared with insect repellent. As if leaving the Transamazonico highway behind, she, the explorer. What beasts would she encounter? It would be better to take along a rifle, food, and water. And a compass. Since having discovered—but having *really* discovered, with a shock—that she would die one day, she had no longer feared life and, thanks to death, now had all her rights: she would risk everything. After having had two relationships that had ended in nothing, this third that had ended in love—adoration, cut short by the fated desire to survive. Eduardo had transformed her: he had given her eyes within. But now she was looking out. Through the window, she saw the mountains, the breasts of the earth. Little birds exist, Eduardo! Clouds exist, Eduardo! There is a world of stallions and mares, and cows, Eduardo, and when I was a girl I raced bareback on a horse, without a saddle! I am fleeing my suicide, Eduardo. I'm sorry, Eduardo, but I don't want to die. I want to be fresh and rare as a pomegranate.

The old woman pretended to be reading the newspaper. But she was thinking: her world was a sigh. She didn't want the others to suppose that she was abandoned. God gave me good health so that I could travel alone. Also my mind is sound, I don't talk to myself, and I bathe on my own every day. She smelled of rose water, of withered macerated roses, her aged and musty perfume. That rhythmic respiration, thought Angela of the old woman, was the most beautiful thing remaining to Dona Maria Rita from her birth. It was life.

Dona Maria Rita was thinking: after getting old, she had begun to disappear for others, had become a passing glimpse. Old age: the supreme moment. She was a stranger to the general strategy of the world and her own was negligible. She had lost the longest-range objectives. She was, in fact, already the future.

Angela thought: I think that if I were to find the truth, I wouldn't be able to think it. It would be mentally unpronounceable.

The old woman had always been a bit empty, a little bit, anyway. Death? It was strange, it wasn't part of the passing days. And even "not to exist" didn't exist, it was impossible not-to-exist. Not to exist didn't fit into our daily life. Her daughter wasn't loving. On the other hand, her son was very loving, good-natured, a bit chubby. The daughter was as bone dry as her rapid little kisses, "public relations." The old woman had a certain laziness about living. It was monotony, however, that sustained her.

Eduardo listened to music with his thoughts. And he understood the dissonance of modern music, he only knew how to understand. His intelligence smothered her. You are temperamental, Angela, he said to her once. And so? What's wrong with that? I am what I am and not what you think I am. The proof that I am is in the departure of this train. My proof is also Dona Maria Rita, there across from me. Proof of what? Yes. She had already had plenitude. When she and Eduardo had been so passionately in love that being beside each other in bed, holding hands, they had felt their lives complete. Few people have known plenitude. And since plenitude is also an explosion, she and Eduardo had, like cowards, begun to live "normally." For you cannot prolong the ecstasy without dying. They had separated for a frivolous, almost artificial reason: they didn't want to die of passion. Plenitude is one of the truths you encounter. But the necessary break was surgery for her, just as there are women whose uteruses and ovaries have been removed. Empty within.

Dona Maria Rita was so ancient that in her daughter's house they were accustomed to her as if to an old piece of furniture. She was news to no one. But it never entered her head that she was a solitary. Just that she had nothing to do. It was an enforced leisure that at times pierced her to the bone: she had nothing to do in the world. Just live like a cat or a dog. She wished she could be an attentive companion to some lady, but such things didn't exist anymore, and anyway no one would believe in her strength at seventy-seven. They would all think she was weak. She didn't do anything, she only did this: to be old. Sometimes she would get depressed: she would feel that she was of no use, no use even to God. Dona Maria Ritinha didn't have an inferno within. Why is it that the old, even those who don't tremble, suggest something delicately tremulous? Dona Maria Rita had a brittle trembling like the music from a hurdy-gurdy.

But when it's a question of life itself—who can shore us up? for each one is a one. And each life has to be supported by its own life, only that one. Each one of us: that's all we can count on. Since Dona Maria Rita had always been an ordinary person, she thought that to die was not a normal thing. To die was surprising. It was as if she wasn't up to the act of death, since until now nothing extraordinary in life had happened to her that could justify all of a sudden another extraordinary event. She spoke and even thought about death, but deep down she was skeptical and suspicious. She believed that you died when there was an accident or when someone killed someone. The old woman had little experience. Sometimes she had palpitations: the heart's bacchanal. But that's all, and it had been with her since girlhood. At her first kiss, for example, her heart had gone out of control. And it had been a good thing alongside the bad. It was something that recalled her past, not as events, but as life: a sensation of vegetation in shadows, ferns, maidenhair, green coolness. When she felt this anew, she smiled. One of the most erudite words she used was "picturesque." It was good. It was like hearing the bubbling of a spring and not knowing where it had its source.

A conversation she carried on with herself:

"Are you doing something?"

"Yes, I am: I'm being sad."

"Doesn't it disturb you to be alone?"

"No, I'm thinking."

Sometimes she didn't think. Sometimes a person just is. She didn't need to be doing. To be was already a doing. One could *be* slowly or somewhat quickly.

On the seat behind, two women talked and talked without end. Their continuous sound mingled with the noise of the train wheels on the tracks.

Indeed, Dona Maria Rita had hoped that her daughter would remain on the platform to give her a little farewell, but it hadn't happened. The train immobile. Until the first lurch came.

"Angela," she said, "a woman never tells her age, so I can only tell you that I am very old. But no, for you—may I speak this way?—I'll tell you a secret: I am seventy-seven years old."

"I'm thirty-seven," said Angela Pralini.

It was seven in the morning.

"When I was young I was quite a little liar. I would lie for nothing just like that."

Later, as if she had become disenchanted with the magic of lies, she had stopped lying.

Angela, looking at old Dona Maria Rita, was afraid of growing old and dying. Hold my hand, Eduardo, so that I won't fear death. But he never held anything. The only thing he did was: think, think, and think. Oh, Eduardo, I need the gentleness of Schumann! Her life was dissolving, an evanescent life. She lacked hard bone, rough and strong, against which no one could do a thing. Who would be that essential bone? To keep at bay her feeling of enormous need, she thought: how did they manage to live in the Middle Ages without telephone and airplane? A mystery. Middle Ages, I adore you, you and your black-laden clouds that streamed into the luminous and fresh Renaissance.

As for the old woman, she had retreated. She was staring at nothingness.

Angela gazed at herself in her little pocket mirror. I look like a swoon. Beware the abyss, I say to the one who looks like a swoon. When I die I will have such a longing for you, Eduardo! The sentence could not stand up to logic, though there was an improbable sense to it. It was as if she had wished to express one thing and had expressed another.

The old woman was already the future. She seemed ashamed. Ashamed of being old? At some point in her life there surely must have been a mistake, and the result was this strange state she was in. Which, however, had not carried her to death. Death was always such a surprise for the one who died. She was, however, proud that she didn't dribble or make weewee in her

bed, as if this form of brute health had been the merito-
rious result of an act of her will. Only she wasn't a lady,
an elderly lady, for she had no arrogance: she was a
dignified little old creature who suddenly would take
on a frightened look. She—well, then, she praised her
very self, considering herself an old woman full of pre-
cocity like a precocious child. But the true purpose of
her life, that she did not know.

Angela dreamed of the farm: there you heard cries,
barks, and howling at night. Eduardo, she thought to
him, I was tired of trying to be what you assumed I was.
I have a bad side—it is the stronger, and it prevailed,
although I tried to hide it because of you—on this
strong side I'm a cow. I'm a mare running free who
paws the ground, I'm a woman of the streets, I'm a
slut—and not a "woman of letters." I know that I am
intelligent and that sometimes I hide it in order not to
offend others with my intelligence, I who am of the
subconscious. I fled from you, Eduardo, because you
were killing me with your genius—intellect that practically forced me to cover my ears with my hands and
scream out in horror and exhaustion. And now I will
remain six months on the farm, you don't know where
I'll be, and every day I'll bathe in the river, mixing with
its clay my own blessed mud. I am vulgar, Eduardo! I
want you to know that I like to read true romance
magazines, my love, oh my love! how I love you and
how I love your terrifying spells, ah, how I adore you,
your slave, slave that I am. But I am physical, my love,
I am physical, and I had to hide from you the glory of
being physical. And you, who are the very splendor of
rational thought, though you don't know it, you were
nourished by me. You, superintellectual and brilliant,
leaving everyone filled with wonder, mouths agape.

I believe, the old woman said to herself slowly, I believe that that pretty girl is not interested in talking to me. I don't know why, but no one speaks with me anymore. And even when I am right there with people, they seem not to remember me. And after all, it's not my fault I'm old. But it doesn't matter, I'll keep myself company. And I still have Nandinho, my dear son who adores me.

The long-suffering pleasure of scratching oneself! thought Angela. I, eh, I who don't go for this or for that, am free!!! I'm getting healthier, oh to swear out loud and startle everyone. Wouldn't the old lady understand? I don't know, she must have given birth a few times. Unhappiness is the only certainty—I'm not going to fall for that, Eduardo. I want to savor everything and then die and may I be damned! damned! damned! Though the old woman may in fact be unhappy without knowing it. Passivity. I'm not going to fall for that either, no passivity for me. I want to bathe naked in the muddy river that looks like me, naked and free! Viva! Three vivas! I'm leaving everything behind! everything! and therefore I am not abandoned, I don't want to depend on anyone but some three people and as for the rest: Hello, how are you? O.K. Edu, you know? I'm leaving you. You, in the depths of your intellectualism, aren't worth the life of a dog. I'm leaving you, then. And I'm leaving the pseudo-intellectual group that demanded of me an unending vain and nervous exercise of a false and hurried intelligence. I needed for God to abandon me before I could feel his presence. I need to kill someone within me. You ruined my intelligence with yours, which is that of a genius. And you forced me to know, to know, to know. Ah, Eduardo, don't worry, I'm taking along the books you gave me in order "to do a home study course," as you wished. I will study philosophy beside the river, for the love I bear you.

Angela Pralini had such deep thoughts that there were no words to express them. It was a lie to say that one could only have one thought at a time: she had numerous thoughts that crossed each other, and they were all different. Not to mention the "subconscious" that explodes in me, whether I want it or you don't. I'm a fountain, thought Angela, thinking at the same time where she had put her kerchief, wondering whether the dog had drunk the milk she had left for him, thinking of Eduardo's shirts, and of his extreme physical and mental exhaustion. And of old Dona Maria Rita. I will never forget your face, Eduardo. It was a somewhat surprised face, surprised at its own intelligence. He was ingenuous. And he loved without knowing that he loved. He would be stunned when he discovered that she had gone off, leaving the dog and him. I'm leaving for lack of nourishment, she thought. At the same time she was thinking of the old lady seated across from her. It wasn't true that you thought only one thought at a time. She was able, for example, to write a perfect check, without an error, while thinking of her life. Which wasn't a good one but at least was hers. Hers once again. Coherence, I don't want it anymore. Coherence is mutilation. I want disorder. I only sense through a vehement incoherence. In order to meditate I draw myself before myself and feel the emptiness. It is in emptiness that time passes. She who loved a good beach, with sun, sand and sun. The man is abandoned, he has lost contact with the earth, with the sky. He no longer lives, he exists. The atmosphere between her and Eduardo Gomes was that of an emergency. He had transformed her into an urgent woman. And, one who, to keep the urgency awake, took drugs, stimulants that made her thinner and thinner and killed her appetite. I want to eat, Eduardo, I'm hungry, Eduardo, I'm hungry for lots of food! I'm organic!

"Meet tomorrow's supertrain today." *Reader's Digests* that she used to read behind Eduardo's back. It was like the *Digests* that said: Meet tomorrow's supertrain today. She was positively not meeting it today. But Eduardo was the supertrain. Super everything. She knew today the super of tomorrow. And she couldn't stand it. She couldn't stand the perpetual motion. You are the desert, and I'm going to Oceania, to the South Seas, to Tahiti. Even if it's ruined by tourism. You are no more than a tourist, Eduardo. I am going toward my own life, Edu. And I say, like Fellini: in darkness and ignorance I create more. The life she had with Eduardo smelled like a newly painted pharmacy. She preferred the living smell of manure no matter how nauseating it might be. He was as proper as a tennis court. In fact, he played tennis to keep in shape. When all was said and done, he was a bore, whom she used to love and almost loved no longer. She was recovering here in the train itself her mental health. She remained in love with Eduardo. And he, unknowingly, with her as well. I who can't manage to do anything right, except make omelettes. With one hand alone I would break eggs with incredible speed, and empty them into the bowl without spilling a drop. Eduardo would die of envy before such elegance and efficiency. He sometimes gave lectures at universities, and they adored him. She, too, attended; she, too, adored him. How was it exactly that he began? "I feel ill at ease seeing people rise upon hearing that I am about to speak." Angela always was afraid that the others would withdraw, leaving them alone.

The old woman, as if she had received a thought

transmission, thought: may they not leave me alone. How old am I really? Humph, I don't even remember.

Quickly, then, she emptied her mind. And she was peacefully nothing. Barely existing. It was good like that, really very good. Plunges into nothingness.

Angela Pralini, in order to calm herself, told herself a most calming, most tranquil story: once upon a time there was a man who loved the jaboticaba fruit. So he went to an orchard where there were trees covered with black protuberances, smooth and glistening, which fell with abandon into his hands and from his hands spilled down to his feet. The jaboticaba berries were so abundant that he gave himself the luxury of stepping on them. And they made a most delicious sound. They went: cloc-cloc-cloc etc. Angela calmed down like the jaboticaba man. On the farm they had jaboticaba, and she would make a moist and soft cloc-cloc-cloc with her bare feet. She never knew whether or not you ought to swallow the pits. Who would answer that question? No one. Only perhaps a man who, like Ulysses the dog, and unlike Eduardo, would answer: "Mangia, bella, que te fa bene." She knew a bit of Italian but was never sure of being right. And, after the man spoke those words, she would swallow the pits. Another delicious tree was one whose scientific name she had forgotten but which, in childhood, everyone had known quite directly, without science, one which in the Botanical Garden in Rio made a dry little cloc-cloc. See? See how you are being reborn? A cat's seven breaths. The number seven always accompanied her, was her secret, her strength. She felt beautiful. She wasn't. But that's how she felt. She also felt generous. With tenderness for old Maria Ritinha, who had put on her glasses and was reading the paper. Everything was slow about old Maria Rita. Near her end? ah, how it hurts to die. In life one suffers, but you have something in your hand: ineffable life. But what about the question of death? You had to have no fear: to go forward, always.

Always.

Like the train.

Somewhere there is something written on a wall. And it is for me, thought Angela. From the flames of hell a fresh telegram will come for me. And never again will my hopes be deceived. Never. Never again.

The old woman was as anonymous as a hen, as a certain Clarice had said speaking of a shameless old woman, madly in love with Roberto Carlos. That Clarice made you uncomfortable. She made the old woman cry out: there must be a way o u t ! And there was, too. For example, the way out for that old lady was her husband, who would return the next day, her acquaintances, her housemaid, intense and fruitful prayer in the face of despair. Angela repeated to herself as if madly biting herself: there must be a way out. For me just as well as for Dona Maria Rita.

I could not stop time, thought Maria Rita Alvarenga Chagas Sousa Melo. I failed. I am old. And she pretended to read the newspaper just to give herself composure.

I need shadows, moaned Angela. I need shadows and anonymity.

The old woman thought: her son was so kind, so warm-hearted, so gentle! He called her "Mom." Yes, perhaps I'll spend the rest of my life on the farm, far from "public relations," who doesn't need me. And my life ought to be very long, to judge by my parents and grandparents. I could easily, easily, reach a hundred, she thought comfortably. And die suddenly in order not to have time to feel fear. She crossed herself discreetly and begged God for a good death.

Ulysses, if his face were seen from a human point of view, would be monstrous and ugly. He was lovely from a dog's point of view. He was filled with vigor like a horse, white and free, only he was a soft brown, orangeish, whiskey-color. But his coat was beautiful like that of an energetic, prancing horse. The muscles of his neck were vigorous, and you could hold those muscles in your hands with knowing fingers. Ulysses was a man. Without a dog's world. He was gentle like a man. A woman must treat a man well.

The train coming to the fields: the crickets cricketing, high pitched and shrill.

Eduardo, once in a while, awkwardly, like someone forced to fulfill a function—would present her with the gift of an icy, uncut, diamond stone. She who preferred them cut. Well, she sighed, things are as they are. At times, looking down from her apartment, she had felt like killing herself. Ah, not because of Eduardo, but because of a kind of fatal curiosity. She wouldn't tell this to anyone, for fear of influencing a latent suicide. She wanted life, life flat and full, really nice, reading *Reader's Digest* for all to see. She wanted to die at ninety, not before, in the middle of an act of life, without feeling a thing. The ghost of madness stalks us. What are you doing? I am awaiting the future.

When the train had finally set in motion, Angela Pralini had lit her cigarette in hallelujah: she had feared before the train had left that she wouldn't have the courage to go and would end up getting off. But after a bit they had become aware of the action of shock-absorbers and, despite this, the sudden jolts of the wheels. The train was moving. And old Maria Rita sighed: she was closer to her beloved son. With him she could be a mother, she who was castrated by her daughter.

Once when Angela had had menstrual cramps, Eduardo had tried, quite awkwardly, to comfort her. And he had said something horrid to her: It was enough to make you blush with shame. You've got a tummy ache, don't you?

The train rushed on as fast as it could. The engineer delighted: this is the good life, and he blew the whistle at every curve. It was the long, heavy whistle of a train underway, clicking off the miles. The morning was cool and full of high green grasses. Yes, that's the way, onward, onward, said the engineer to the engine. The engine responded joyfully.

The old woman was nothing. And gazed into the air as one looks at God. She was made of God. That is, of all or nothing. The old woman was vulnerable, Angela thought. Vulnerable to love, love of her son. The mother was Franciscan, the daughter pollution.

God, thought Angela, if you exist, reveal yourself! For the hour has come. It is this hour, this minute, and this second.

And the result was that she had to hide the tears that came to her eyes. God in some way had answered her. She was happy and swallowed a muffled sob. How painful life was. Living was an open wound. To live is to be like my dog. Ulysses has nothing in common with Joyce's Ulysses. I tried to read Joyce, but I stopped because he was boring, sorry, Eduardo. Only he's a boring genius. Angela was feeling love for the old woman who was nothing, the mother she lacked. A mother, gentle, ingenuous, long-suffering. Her mother who had died when she was nine years old. Even sick, just being alive was enough. Even paralyzed.

Between her and Eduardo the air tasted like Saturday. And suddenly the two of them were rare, a rarity in the air. They felt rare, apart from the thousand people walking in the streets. At times the two were accomplices, they had a secret life because no one would have understood them. And also because rare ones are persecuted by the people who do not tolerate the insulting offence of those who are different. They hid their love in order not to wound the eyes of others with envy. In order not to wound them with a spark too luminous for eyes.

Bowwow wow, yapped my dog. My big puppy.

The old woman thought: I am an involuntary person. So much so that when she laughed—which was rare—you didn't know if she were laughing or crying. Yes. She was involuntary.

Meanwhile Angela Pralini, fizzling like the bubbles in Caxamba mineral water, was one too: all of a sudden. Just like that. All of a sudden what? Just all of a sudden. Zero. Nothing. She was thirty-seven years old and always intending to begin her life anew. Like the fizzling effervescent bubbles of Caxamba water. The seven letters of Pralini gave her strength. The six letters of Angela made her anonymous.

With a drawn-out wailing whistle, they arrived at the small station where Angela Pralini was going to jump out. She picked up her suitcase. In the space between the porter's cap and the nose of a young woman, there was the old lady sleeping, inflexible, her head priggishly erect beneath its felt hat, her fist closed over the newspaper.

Angela stepped down from the train.

Naturally this hadn't the slightest importance: there

are people who always tend to regret, it's a trait of certain guilty natures. But the vision of the old woman waking up, the image of her face, surprised by Angela's empty seat, began to disturb her. In the end no one could know if she had fallen asleep thanks to her trust in Angela.

Trust in the world.

DRY POINT OF HORSES

DESPOILMENT

The horse—naked.

FICTITIOUS DOMESTICATION

What is horse? It is freedom so indomitable that it
becomes useless to imprison it to serve man: it lets itself
be domesticated, but with a simple, rebellious toss of
the head—shaking its mane like an abundance of free-
flowing hair—it shows that its inner nature is always
wild, translucent, and free.

FORM

The form of the horse exemplifies what is best in the
human being. I have a horse within me who rarely
reveals himself. But when I see another horse, then
mine expresses himself. His form speaks.

GENTLENESS

What makes a horse be of glistening satin? It is the
gentleness of one who has taken on life and its rainbow.
This gentleness manifests itself in a smooth coat, sug-
gesting elastic muscles, agile and controlled.

THE EYES OF THE HORSE

I once saw a blind horse: nature had erred. It was painful to feel him so restless, aware of the slightest sound caused by the breeze amongst the grasses, with his nerves ready to bristle in a shudder running throughout his alert body. What does a horse see so that not seeing his kind leaves him as if having lost his very self? It's just that when he looks, he sees outside himself what is inside himself. He is an animal who expresses himself through form. When he sees mountains, meadows, people, the sky—he takes dominion over men and over nature itself.

SENSITIVITY

All horses are wild and skittish when unsure hands touch them.

HE AND I

Trying to formulate my most hidden and subtle sensations—and disobeying an exigent need for truth—I would say: if I could have chosen, I would have wished to be born a horse. But—who knows—maybe the horse himself doesn't sense that great symbol of free life which we sense in him. Must I then conclude that the horse is there above all to be felt by me? Does the horse represent the beautiful and free animality of human beings? The best of the horse—does the human creature already have it? Then I abdicate being a horse and with glory pass on to my humanity. The horse tells me what I am.

THE ADOLESCENCE OF THE YOUNG GIRL-COLT

I already got along perfectly with horses. I remember myself as me-adolescent. Standing straight with the same haughtiness as the horse and passing my hand over his glistening hide. Through his aggressive, rugged mane. I felt as if something of me were seeing us from far away: "The Girl and the Horse."

DISPLAY

On the ranch, the white horse—the king of nature— hurled through the heights of the keen air his drawn-out whinny of splendor.

THE DANGEROUS HORSE

In the little country town—which would become a small metropolis one day—horses still reigned as the leading inhabitants. Due to the increasingly urgent need for transportation, droves of horses had invaded the hick town, and in the still-wild children there stirred the secret desire to gallop. A young bay gave a fatal kick to a boy who was mounting him. And the place where the daring child had died was regarded with censure by people who, in fact, didn't know at whom to direct it. With their shopping baskets on their arms, women would stop to stare. A newspaper took up the case, and, with a certain pride, you could read a brief notice under the title "The Horse's Crime." It was the Crime of one of the sons of that little town. The burg by then was mixing with its smell of stables an awareness of the strength bound within a horse.

ON THE SUN-BAKED STREET

But suddenly—in the silence of the two o'clock sun, with almost no one on the straggling streets—a pair of horses surged around a corner. For a moment they stood motionless, their hooves half raised. Gleaming at the mouth, as if unmuzzled. There, like statues. The

few passers-by daring to face the heat of the sun gazed
at them, hard, isolated, without understanding in
words what they saw. They just understood. The obfus-
cation of the apparition gone, the horses arched their
necks, lowered their hooves, and continued on their
way. The moment of recognition had passed. A moment fixed as if by a camera that has captured something which words will never say.

IN THE SETTING SUN

That day, as the sun was going down, gold spilled
through the clouds and over the rocks. The faces of the
townsfolk turned golden like armor and their flowing
hair gleamed as well. Dust-covered factories gave forth
prolonged whistles marking the end of the workday, a
wagon wheel took on a gilded nimbus. In this gold,
pallid from the breeze, there was a raising of an un-
sheathed sword. For that's how the equestrian statue of
the square loomed in the softness of nightfall.

IN THE COLD DAWN

You could see the warm, moist breath—the radiant and
peaceful breath that came from the tremulous, life-
filled, flaring nostrils of stallions and mares in the cold
of certain dawns.

IN THE MYSTERY OF NIGHT

But at night, horses released from their burdens and led
to pasture would gallop lithe and free in the darkness.
Colts, old nags, sorrels, long-legged mares, hardened
hooves—suddenly a horse's head, cold and dark!—
hooves pounding, frothy muzzles rising toward the air,
enraged and murmuring. And sometimes a deep breath
would chill the trembling blades of grass. Then the bay

would come forward. He would walk sideways, head curved down to his chest, in a gentle cadence. The others attended without looking. Hearing the sound of the horses, I could imagine their dry hooves advancing, till coming to a halt at the highest point on the hill. And the head, dominating the little town, throwing out a long-drawn whinny. Fear gripped me in the shadows of my room, the fear of a king. I would have liked, gums bare, to give a whinny in response. In the envy of desire, my face took on the anxious nobility of a horse's head. Exhausted, jubilant, listening to the somnambulist trot. As soon as I left my room, my shape would start to fill out and purify, and by the time I reached the street, I would be galloping on sensitive feet, my hooves slipping at the bottom of the front steps. From the deserted pavement I would look around: one corner and the other. And I would see things as a horse sees them. That was what I wanted. From the house I would try, at least, to listen to the hillside pasture where, in the darkness, nameless horses were galloping, returned to a world of the hunt and of war.

The beasts did not abandon their secret life that goes on during the night. And if in the midst of the wild, milling herd a white colt appeared—it was wonderment in the dark. They all would stop in their tracks. The prodigious horse would *appear*, an apparition. It would show itself rearing for an instant. Immobile, the animals would wait, not looking at each other. But one of them would strike his hoof—and the sharp blow would break the vigil: whipped up, they would suddenly move with a new vigor, interweaving without any bumping, and among them the white horse would be lost. Until a whinny of sudden rage alerted them— intent for a moment, they quickly fanned out once again, trotting in a new formation, their backs without horsemen, their necks so low their muzzles touched their chests. Their manes bristling. And they, cadenced, uncivilized.

Late night—while men were sleeping—would find them motionless in the dark. Solid and without weight. There they were, invisible, breathing. Waiting with their limited intelligence. Below, in the sleeping village, a cock fluttered up and settled on a window sill. The hens looked at him. Beyond the railroad tracks a rat ready to flee. Then the dapple struck his hoof. He had no mouth to speak with, but he produced that small sign which surfaced now and then in the darkness. They looked about. Those animals with an eye for looking both ways at once—nothing had to be seen head-on by them, and that was the great night. The flanks of a mare rippled with rapid contractions. In the silence of the night, the mare gazed out as if surrounded by eternity. The most restless colt was still raising its mane in a muffled whinny. And then utter silence reigned.

Until the fragile luminosity of dawn revealed them. They were separate, standing on the hill. Exhausted, fresh. They had passed through the mystery of the nature of living beings, there in the darkness.

STUDY OF THE DIABOLIC HORSE

I will never rest easy again, for I have stolen the hunting horse of a King. Now I am worse than I myself! I will never rest easy again: I stole the King's hunting horse on the witching sabbath. If I fall asleep for a moment, the echo of a whinny awakens me. And it is useless to try not to go. In the dark of the night, a snorting makes me shiver. I pretend to be sleeping, but in the silence the jennet breathes. Every day it will be the same: already as the afternoon lengthens I begin to turn melancholy and pensive. I know that the first drum on the mountain of evil will make the night, I know that the third will have already enveloped me in its thunder. And at the fifth drum, I will be filled with desire for a ghost horse. Until at dawn, to the last and softest drumbeats, I will find myself, not knowing how, beside a fresh little stream, never knowing what I have done, next to the enormous tired head of a horse.

But tired from what? What did we do, I and the horse, we who trot in the hell of the vampire's joy? He, the King's steed, calls me. I have resisted in a bout of sweat and won't go. The last time I descended from his silver saddle, my human sadness at having been what shouldn't have been was so great that I swore—never again. The trot, however, continues inside me. I talk, straighten up the house, smile, but I know that the trot is inside me. I miss him like someone dying.

No, I cannot help but go.

And I know that at night, when he calls me, I will go. I want the horse to lead my thoughts one more time. It was with him that I learned. If this is thought, this hour between yelpings. I begin to grow sad because I know through my eyes—oh, without wanting to! it isn't my fault—with my eyes involuntarily resplendent now with evil glee—I know that I will go.

When at night he calls me to hell's allurements, I will go. I descend like a cat along the rooftops. No one knows, no one sees. Only dogs bark, sensing the supernatural.

And I present myself in the dark to the horse who awaits me, horse of royalty, I present myself in silence and in splendor. Obedient to the Beast.

Fifty-three flutes run after us. In front, a clarinet

lights the way for us, shameless accomplices of the enigma. And nothing more is given me to know.

At dawn I will see us exhausted beside the little stream, without knowing what crimes we committed before reaching innocent dawn.

In my mouth and on his hooves the mark of great blood. What is it we have sacrificed?

At dawn I will be standing next to the jennet, now still, with the rest of the flutes still dripping from my hair. The first churchbells from afar make us shiver and set us in flight, we dissolve before the cross.

The night is my life with the diabolic horse, I, witch of horror. The night is my life, it grows late, the sin-fully happy night is the sad life that is my orgy—ah steal, steal from me the jennet, for from robbery to robbery even dawn I have stolen for myself and for my fantastical partner, and I have turned the dawn into a presentiment of the terror of demoniacal, un-wholesome joy.

Free me, quickly steal the jennet while there is time, before it is too late, while there is still day without darkness, if indeed there still is time, for in stealing the jennet I had to kill the King, and killing him I stole the King's death. And the orgiastic joy of our murder con-sumes me in terrible pleasure. Quickly steal the King's perilous horse, steal him, steal me, before night falls and calls for me.

WHERE YOU WERE AT NIGHT

"Stories have no resolution."

Alberto Dines

"The unknown corrupts."

Fauzi Arap

"Sitting in an armchair, with a mouth full of teeth, waiting for death."

Raul Seixas

"What I am about to announce is so new that I fear I will have all men as enemies, to such an extent do preconceptions and doctrines take root, once they are accepted."

William Harvey

The night offered exceptional possibility. In the midst of darkest night, during a scalding summer, a rooster gave forth an unscheduled cry, just once, to announce the start of the climb up the mountain. The crowd below waited in silence.

He-she was already there at the top of the mountain, and she was personified in the he and he was personified in the she. The androgynous mixture had created a being so terribly beautiful, so horrifyingly stupefying, that the participants could not look at it all at once:

just like a person bit by bit getting used to the dark and beginning to make things out. Slowly they began to make out the She-he, and when the He-she appeared to them with a clarity emanating from her-him, paralyzed by what was Beauty, they would say: "Ah, ah." It was an exclamation that was allowed in the silence of the night. They gazed at the frightening beauty and its danger. But they had come precisely in order to suffer that danger.

The swamps were exhaling. A star of great density was guiding them. They were the Good inside-out. They climbed the mountain mixing men, women, elves, gnomes, and dwarves—like extinct gods. The golden bell tolled for the suicides. Except for the enormous star, no other star at all. And there was no sea. What there was atop the mountain was darkness. A wind was blowing from the northwest. Was He-she a beacon? The adoration of the damned was about to take place.

The men wriggled on the ground like thick, soft worms: they were climbing. They were risking everything, since inevitably one day they would die, perhaps in two months, perhaps in seven years—it was this that He-she was thinking within them.

Look at the cat. Look at what the cat saw. Look at what the cat thought. Look at what it was. Finally, finally, there wasn't a symbol, there was the "thing," the orgiastic thing. Those who were climbing were on the verge of the truth. Nebuchadnezzar. They seemed like twenty Nebuchadnezzars. And in the night they separated. They are waiting for us. It was an absence —a voyage outside of time.

A dog howled with laughter in the dark. "I'm scared," said the child. "Scared of what?" asked the mother. "Of my dog." "But you don't have a dog." "Yes I do." But later on, the little child also burst out crying and chortling, mixing tears of laughter and amazement.

Finally they arrived, the damned. And they looked at that eternal Widow, the great Recluse who fascinated everyone, and the men and women couldn't resist and wanted to get closer to her in order to love her as they were dying, but she held them all at a distance with a single gesture. They wanted to love her with a strange love that quivers in death. It didn't disturb them to love her as they were dying. She-he's cloak was of the pained color violet. But the mercenaries of sex, so festive, tried in vain to imitate her.

What time might it be? no one could live in time, time was indirect and by its very nature always unreachable. They already had swollen joints, debris rumbled in stomachs filled with earth, their lips were tumescent, yet fissured—they were climbing the slope. The blackness was of a sound low and dark, like the darkest note of a cello. They had arrived. The Ill-Fated, the He-she, before the adoration of kings and vassals, sparkled like a gigantic illuminated eagle. The silence swarmed with panting breaths. The vision was of mouths half open with a sensuality which almost paralyzed them with its heaviness. They felt themselves saved from the Great Boredom.

The hill was a scrap heap. When the She-he stopped for a moment, men and women, left to themselves for a moment, frightened, said to one another: I don't know how to think. But the He-she was thinking within them.

A mute herald with a sharp clarinet announced the news. What news? news of bestiality? Perhaps it was just this: from the herald on, they all began to "feel," to feel themselves. And there was no repression: they were free!

And then they began to murmur, but within, for the She-he was vitriolic about their not disturbing one another in their slow metamorphosis. "I am Jesus! I am Jewish!" cried the poor Jew in silence. The annals of astronomy had never registered anything like this spectacular comet, recently discovered—its vaporous tail will drag along through millions of miles in space. Not to mention time.

A hunchbacked dwarf was hopping about like a toad, from one crossroad to another—the place was full of crossroads. Suddenly stars appeared, and they were gems and diamonds in the dark sky. And the dwarf-hunchback made leaps as high as he could go to reach the diamonds his greed was awakening. Crystals! Crystals! he cried in thoughts that were tripping about like the leaps themselves.

Latency was throbbing, light, rhythmic, uninterrupted. They all were everything in latency. "There is no crime we have not committed in our thoughts": Goethe. A new and inauthentic Brazilian story had been written abroad. Besides that, national researchers complained of a lack of resources for their work.

The mountain was of volcanic origin. And suddenly the sea: the turbulent breaking of the Atlantic filled their ears. And the salt smell of the sea fertilized them and triplicated them into little monsters.

Can the human body fly? Levitation. St. Teresa of Avila: "It seemed as if a great force was lifting me into the air. This provoked a great fear in me." The dwarf levitated for a few seconds, but he liked it and he was not afraid.

"What is your name," the boy said silently, "so I can

call for you throughout my life. I will cry out your name."

"I have no name down there. Here I have the name Xanthippe."

"Ah, I want to cry out Xanthippe! Xanthippe! Look, I'm crying out within. And what is your name in the daytime?"

"I think it's . . . it's . . . it seems to be Maria Luisa."

And she shivered the way a horse bristles. She fell, bloodless, to the ground. No one was murdering anyone, for they were already murdered. No one wished to die and, in fact, they didn't die.

Meanwhile—delicately, delicately—the He-she was employing a certain tone. The color of a tone. For I want to live in plenty, and I would betray my best friend in exchange for more life than one can have. This searching, this ambition. I despised the precepts of those sages who counsel moderation and poverty of spirit—the simplification of the soul, according to my own experience, was holy innocence. But I struggled against temptation.

Yes, yes: to fall to utter debasement. *That* is their ambition. The sound was the herald of silence. For not one of them could allow himself to be possessed by that He-She-without-name.

They wanted to savor the forbidden. They wanted to praise life and did not want the pain that is necessary for living, for feeling, and for loving. They wanted to feel terrifying immortality. For the forbidden is always the best. At the same time, it didn't bother them that they might fall into the enormous pit of death. And life was only precious to them when they screamed and moaned. To feel the strength of hatred was what they desired most. My name is people, they thought.

"What must I do to become a hero?" For only heroes enter the temples.

And in the silence, suddenly, his howling cry, one didn't know if of love or mortal pain, the hero smelling of myrrh, frankincense, and benjamin.

He-she covered his nakedness with a cloak, lovely but like a shroud, a purple shroud, now cathedral-red. On moonless nights, She-he turned into a screech owl. You will eat your brother, she said in the thoughts of others, and at the savage hour there will be an eclipse of the sun.

In order not to betray themselves, they ignored the fact that today was yesterday and there would be a tomorrow. There wafted through the air a transparency the like of which no man had ever breathed before. But they sprinkled powdered pepper on their own genitals and writhed with the heat. And suddenly hatred. They did not kill each other, but felt such implacable hatred that it was like a spear thrown into a body. And they grew jubilant, damned by what they felt. Hatred was a vomit that released them from a greater vomit, the vomit of the soul.

He-she, with the seven musical notes, brought forth the howl. Just as with the same seven notes it could have created sacred music. They heard within themselves the do-re-mi-fa-sol-la-ti, the "ti" soft and very high. They were independent and sovereign, in spite of being led by the He-she. Roaring death in the dark holds. Fire, scream, color, vice, cross. I am careful in the world: at night I live and during the day I sleep, elusive. I, like a dog on the scent, orgiastic.

As for them, they carried out rituals that the faithful execute without understanding their mysteries. The ceremony. With a light motion, She-he touched a child, annihilating it, and everyone said: amen. The mother howled like a wolf: she, utterly dead, she, too.

But it was to have supersensations that one climbed

up there. And it was a sensation so secret and so deep that the jubilation sparkled in the air. They wanted the superior force that has reigned in the world through the centuries. Were they afraid? They were. Nothing took the place of the richness of silent dread. To fear was the cursed glory of the darkness, silent as a Moon.

Bit by bit they got used to the dark, and the Moon, hidden until then, all round and pale, had slowed their ascent. It had been utter dark when one by one they had climbed "the mountain," as they called the plateau a bit higher up. They had clung to the slope in order not to fall, stepping on dry and rough trees, stepping on thorny cactus. It was an irresistibly attractive fear, they would rather die than abandon it. The He-she was like the Lover to them. But if one of them, more ambitious, dared to touch her, he was frozen in the very position he was in.

He-she told them in their brains—and they all listened to her within themselves—what would happen to a person who didn't respond to the call of the night: in the blindness of the light of day, the person would live in open flesh and in eyes dazzled by the sin of light—the person would live, without anesthesia, the terror of being alive. There is nothing to fear when you are not afraid. It was the eve of the apocalypse. Who was the king of the Earth? If you abuse the power that you have gained, the masters will punish you. Filled with the terror of a ferocious joy, they sank down and, shrieking with laughter, began to eat weeds from the ground, and their shrieks resounded from darkness to darkness with their echoing. A stifling smell of roses filled the air with heaviness, roses cursed in their own strength by a nature gone mad, the same nature which invented snakes and rats and pearls and children—crazed nature that was either night of utter darkness or day of light. This flesh that moves only because it has spirit.

Thick saliva drooled from their mouths, bitter and greasy, and they pissed on themselves without feeling it. The women who had recently given birth squeezed their own breasts with violence, and from their nipples a thick, black milk squirted forth. A woman spat hard in the face of a man, and the rough spit dripped from his cheek to his mouth—avidly he licked his lips.

They were all cast loose. The joy was frenetic. They were the harem of He-she. They had fallen finally into the impossible. Mysticism had become the highest form of superstition.

The millionaire was screaming: I want power! power! I want objects themselves to obey my orders! And I will say: move over object! and on its own it will move over.

The old disheveled woman said to the millionaire: do you want to see how it is you're not a millionaire? Well, I'll tell you: you don't own the next second of life, you could die without knowing it. Death will humiliate you. The millionaire: I want the truth, the naked truth!

The journalist doing a marvelous article on raw life. I will gain international fame, like the author of *The Exorcist,* which I haven't read so as not to be influenced by it. I'm looking straight at raw life, I'm living it.

I'm a loner, said the masturbator to himself.

I'm in waiting, waiting, nothing ever happens to me, I've already given up waiting. They were drinking the bitter liquor of coarse herbs.

"I'm a prophet! I see the beyond!" a young man shouted to himself.

Father Joaquim Jesus Jacinto—all with the letter J because his mother liked the letter J.

It was the thirty-first of December, 1973. Sidereal time would be measured against atomic clocks, which fall behind by just one second every three thousand three hundred years.

The other one began to sneeze, one sneeze after another, without stopping. But she liked it. Her name was J.B.

"My life is a true romance!" shouted the failed writer.

Ecstasy was reserved for He-she. Who suddenly experienced a prolonged exhaltation of the body. She-he said: stop! For she was being driven mad by feeling the pleasure of Evil. All of them were taking pleasure through her: it was the celebration of the Great Law. The eunuchs did something it was forbidden to see. The others, through She-he, received, quivering, the waves of orgasm—but only waves, for they didn't have the strength to receive it all without destroying themselves. The women painted their mouths purple, as if they were fruit crushed by sharpened teeth.

The She-he told them what would happen if they didn't enter into the prophetics of the night. State of shock. For example: the young woman was a redhead, and as if that weren't enough, she was red inside and, besides that, color-blind. So much so that in her little apartment she had a green cross on a red background: she confused the two colors. How had her terror begun? Listening to a record or to a reigning silence or to footsteps on the floor above—and there she goes, terrified. Afraid of the mirror that reflected her. Opposite her was a wardrobe, and her impression was that the clothes were moving around inside. Bit by bit, she was reducing the apartment. She was even afraid to get out of bed. Had the impression that they would grab her foot from under the bed. She was very thin. Her name was Psiu, a red name. She was afraid of turning on the light in the dark and coming upon the cold little lizard that lived with her. She could feel, in agony, the frozen little white fingers of the lizard. She avidly sought in the newspaper for the crime pages, news of what was going on. Terrifying things were always happening to people who, like her, lived alone and were attacked at night. On the wall she had a picture of a man who stared her straight in the eyes, watching her. She imagined that face following her to all corners of the house. She had a panicky fear of mice. She would have preferred to die than have contact with them. And yet she heard them squeaking. She came to feel them nibbling at her feet. She always awoke with a start, in a cold sweat. She was a cornered creature. Usually she conversed with herself. She presented the pros and the cons, and it was always she who lost. Her life was an on-going subtraction of herself. All this because she didn't respond to the siren's call.

The He-she only allowed you to see the female androgyn face. And from it there irradiated such a blind, insane splendor that the others were able to enjoy madness itself. She was the oracle and dissolution, and she was born already tattooed. All the air smelled now of fatal jasmine, and it was so strong that some vomited forth their very entrails. The Moon was full in the sky. Fifteen thousand adolescents were waiting to see what kind of man and woman they were going to be.

And then She-he said:

"I will eat your brother, and there will follow a total eclipse and the end of the world."

Now and then one would hear a long whinny, but there was no horse to be seen. The only thing one knew was that all the music that exists, that has existed, and that will exist, is made from seven musical notes. From She-he emanated the strong odor of crushed jasmine, for it was the night of the full Moon. Witchcraft and sorcery. Max Ernst, as a child, was mistaken for the Infant Jesus in a procession. Later he provoked artistic scandals. He had a limitless passion for mankind and an immense and poetic freedom. But why am I speaking of this? I don't know. "I don't know" is a wonderful response.

What did Thomas Edison do, so inventive and free, in the midst of those at He-she's command?

Cacography, mused the perfect student, is the most difficult word in the language.

Hark! the herald angels sing!

The poor Jew cried out silently and no one heard him, no one in the whole world heard him. This is what he said: I live with thirst, sweat, and tears! and to sate my thirst I drink my sweat and my own salt tears. I eat no pork! I follow the Torah! But give me relief, Jehovah, for the pig is too much like me!

Jubileu de Almeida listened to his portable radio all the time. "The best tasting porridge is made with Cremogema." And then they announced a waltz by Strauss which, incredible as it might seem, was called "The Freethinker." It's true, it really exists, I've heard it. Jubileu was the owner of "At the Golden Mandolin," a nearly bankrupt shop for musical instruments, and he was crazy about those Strauss waltzes. He was a widower, he was, that is to say Jubileu. His rival was "The Bugle," a competitor on Rua Gomes Freire or Frei Caneca. Jubileu was also a piano tuner.

Everyone there was about to be smitten. Sex. Pure sex. They held themselves back. Rumania was a dangerous country: gypsies.

There wasn't enough oil in the world. And without oil, there wasn't enough food. Meat, especially. And without meat, they were turning terribly carnivorous.

"Here, Lord, I commend my soul to You," said Christopher Columbus, as he lay dying, dressed in a Franciscan habit. He did not eat meat. He hallowed himself. Christopher Columbus, the discoverer of the waves, and the one who discovered St. Francis of Assisi. Hélas! he died. Where are you now? where? for God's sake, answer!

Suddenly and quite gently—*fiat lux.*

There was a nervous scattering, as of sparrows. It was all so quick they seemed simply to have vanished.

At that moment, some were lying in bed asleep, others already awake. What had been was silence. They didn't know a thing. The guardian angels—who had taken a break since everyone was quietly in bed—awoke refreshed, yawning still, but already protecting their charges.

Dawn: the egg came whirling slowly from the horizon into space. It was morning: a young woman, blond, married to a rich fellow, gives birth to a black baby. Son of the demon of the night? No one knows. A pile of troubles, shame.

Jubileu de Almeida awoke like yesterday's bread: stale. Ever since he was little, he had been dried up like this. He turned on the radio and heard: "Morena's Shoes—where high prices are forbidden." He would go there: he needed some shoes. Jubileu was an albino, black steel with yellow, almost white, eyelashes. He broke an egg in the frying pan. And he thought: if I could someday hear Strauss's "The Freethinker," I would be rewarded in my loneliness. He had just heard that waltz once, he couldn't remember when.

The tycoon wanted to eat Danish caviar by the spoonful for "breakfast," bursting the little balls with his sharp teeth. He belonged to the Rotary Club and the Masons and the Diner's Club. He had the refinement of not eating Russian caviar: it was a way of defeating powerful Russia.

The poor Jew wakes up and drinks eagerly, direct from the faucet. It was the only water to be had down in the depths of the dirt-cheap boarding house where he lived: once he had seen a cockroach swimming in the thin bean soup. The prostitutes who lived there didn't even complain.

The perfect student, who didn't suspect he was a real drag, was thinking: what was the most difficult word in existence? What was it? One that suggested adornments, fineries, and fripperies. Ah, yes, cacography. He learned the word by heart in order to write it on the next exam.

When the day began to shine forth, everyone was in bed, yawning endlessly. Upon waking up, one was a shoemaker, one was in prison for rape, one was a housewife, giving orders to a cook, who never arrived late, another was a banker, another a secretary, etc. They woke up, then, a bit tired, satisfied with their deep, deep night of sleep. Saturday had passed, and today was Sunday. And many were at the Mass being celebrated by Father Jacinto, who was all the rage: but no one went to confession, for they had nothing to confess.

The failed writer opened her diary bound in red leather and began to record the following: "7th of July, 1974. I, I, I, I, I, I, I! On this beautiful morning with its Sunday sun, after having slept very badly, I, in spite of everything, appreciate the marvelous beauties of Mother Nature. I don't go to the beach because I am too fat, and that is an unhappiness for someone who appreciates so much the little green waves of the Sea! I rebel! But I cannot manage to diet: I'm dying of hunger. I like living dangerously. Your viperous tongue will be sliced through by the scissors of complacency."

In the morning: agnus dei. Calf of gold? Vulture.

The poor Jew: deliver me from the pride of being a Jew!

The journalist called her friend very early in the morning:

"Claudia, forgive me for calling at such an hour on a Sunday! But I woke up with a fabulous inspiration: I'm going to write a book about Black Magic! No, I didn't read that *Exorcist*, since they told me it was bad literature and I didn't want them to think that I was tagging along in its wake. Do you know what this means? The human being has always tried to communicate with the supernatural, from ancient Egypt with the secret of the pyramids, to Greece with its gods, to Shakespeare with his Hamlet. Well, I'm going to get into it, too. And, by God, I'm going to make it big!"

There was the smell of coffee in many houses in Rio. It was Sunday. And the boy still in bed, filled with drowsiness, still barely awake, said to himself: another Sunday of utter boredom. What did I dream, anyway? Who knows, he replied to himself, if I dreamed, I dreamed of a woman.

Finally, the air lightened. And the everyday began. Crude day. The light was evil: haunted daily day was installing itself. Religion was becoming necessary: a religion that was not afraid of dawn. I want to be envied. I want rape, robbery, infanticide, and this challenge of mine is powerful! I want gold and fame, I have scorned sex: loved quickly and didn't know what love was. I want evil gold. Profanation. I go to the extreme. After the feast—what feast? nocturnal?—after the feast, desolation.

There was the observer who wrote the following in his notebook: "Progress, and all the phenomena that surround it, seems to participate intimately in that law of acceleration, general, cosmic, and centrifugal, which drags civilization to 'maximum progress,' so that after that comes the fall. An uninterrupted fall or a quickly contained fall? That's the problem: we cannot know if this society will destroy itself utterly or will simply encounter a sudden interruption and then a resumption of its forward motion." And then: "The Sun would diminish its effect upon the Earth, provoking the beginning of a new ice age that could last at least ten thousand years." Ten thousand years was a lot, and it was frightening. That's what happens when someone chooses, for fear of the dark night, to live in the superficial light of day. Yes, the supernatural, divine or demonic, has been a temptation since Egypt, passing through the Middle Ages to the dimestore mysteries of today.

The butcher, who on that day only worked from eight to eleven, opened the butcher shop: and stopped, drunk with pleasure at the smell of flesh, raw meat, raw and bloody. He was the only one who during the day continued the night.

Father Jacinto was fashionable because no one else could lift the chalice as limpidly as he, and drink with such sacred unction and purity, saving everyone, the blood of Jesus, who was the Good. With delicacy, the pale hands in a gesture of oblation.

The baker, as always, woke up at four o'clock and began to prepare the dough for bread. At night did he knead the Devil?

An angel painted by Fra Angelico, fifteenth century, fluttered through the air: he was the clarinet announcing morning. The electric streetlights had not yet gone out, and they glowed pallidly. Lampposts. Speed devours the lampposts when one rushes by in a car.

The morning masturbator: my only faithful friend is my dog. He trusts no one, especially not women.

She who had yawned all night long and said: "I cast you forth, Mother Sorceress!" began to scratch and to yawn. Damnation, she said.

The tycoon—who took great care with orchids, cattleya, and oncidium—impatiently rang the buzzer to summon the butler to bring him his already belated breakfast. The butler always guessed his thoughts and knew when to bring him the Great Danes for a quick caress.

The woman who at night cried out "I am waiting, waiting, waiting, waiting," in the morning, totally disheveled, said to the milk in the saucepan on the stove:

"I'll get you, you swine, I want to see if you screw up and boil to my very face, my life is one of waiting. Everyone knows that if I look away from the milk for a moment, the damned thing will grab its chance and boil over. Like death which comes when one doesn't expect it."

She waited, waited, and the milk did not boil. So, she turned off the gas.

In the sky the faintest rainbow: it was the sign. The morning like a white dew. White dove was the prophecy. Manger. Secret. The foreordained morning. Ave Maria, gratia plena, dominus tecum. Benedicta tu in mulieribus et benedictum frutus ventri tui Jesus. Sancta Maria Mater Dei ora pro nobis pecatoribus. Nunca et ora nostrae morte Amen.

Father Jacinto lifted up in his two hands the crystal

chalice that contained the scarlet blood of Christ. Wow, good wine. And a flower was born. A delicate, pink flower, with the fragrance of God. He-she had vanished long before in the air. The morning was crystal clear like something recently washed.

AMEN

The inattentive faithful made the sign of the Cross.

AMEN

GOD

THE END

Epilogue:

All that I have written is true—it exists. There exists a universal mind that has guided me. Where were you at night? No one knows. Don't try to answer—for the love of God. I don't want to know your answer. Adeus. A-Deus.

A REPORT ON A THING

This thing is the hardest thing for a person to understand. Insist. Don't give up. It may appear obvious. But it's very hard to understand. For it concerns time.

We divide time, but in reality it isn't divisible. It is for always and immutable. But we must divide it up. And for this a monstrous thing has been created: the clock.

I'm not going to talk about clocks. Just about one specific clock. My game is out in the open: I say right away what I have to say, and without literary embellishments. This report is the antiliterature of the thing.

The clock of which I speak is electronic, and it has an alarm. The brand is Sveglia, in other words "Wake up!" Wake up for what, for God's sake? For time. For the hour. For the moment. That clock isn't mine. But I have taken possession of its infernal, tranquil soul.

It isn't a wristwatch: therefore it is free. It's an inch tall and stands on the tabletop. I wish it were really called Sveglia. But the owner of the clock wants to call it Horace. It doesn't much matter. For the main thing is that it is time.

Its mechanism is very simple. It doesn't have the complexity of a person, but it's more human than a man. Is it a superman? No, it comes straight from the planet Mars, or so it seems. If that's where it's from, then that's where it'll return some day. It would be foolish to mention that it doesn't need to be wound, since this is also true of other timepieces, like my wrist-watch, which is shock-resistant and can get as wet as you like. That kind is even more than a man! But at least it is of the Earth. The Sveglia is of God. Divine human brains were used to capture what this clock ought to be. I'm writing about it, but I still haven't seen it. The Meeting will take place. Sveglia: wake up, woman, wake up to see what must be seen. It's important to be awake in order to see. But it's also important to sleep in order to dream of the absence of time. Sveglia is the Object, the Thing, with a capital letter. Could it be that Sveglia sees me? Yes, he does, as if I were another object. He realizes that sometimes even people come from Mars.

Things have been happening to me, since first I learned about Sveglia, that seem more like a dream. Wake me up, Sveglia, I want to see reality. But, in fact, reality seems a dream. I am sad because I am happy. This is not a paradox. After the act of love, isn't there a certain sadness? That of plenitude. I would like to cry. Sveglia doesn't cry. Of course he has no reason to. Could it be that his energy has weight? Sleep, Sveglia, sleep a bit, I can't stand your vigil. You never cease to be. You never dream. It cannot be said that you "function": you are not a functioning, you just are.

You are utterly thin. And nothing happens to you. But it is you who makes things happen. Happen to me, Sveglia, happen to me. I need a specific happening about which I cannot speak. And give me back desire, the mainspring of animal life. I don't want you for myself. I don't like being watched. And you are the only eye that is always open like an eye floating in space. You don't wish me ill; nor, however, do you wish me well. Could it be that I also am becoming like that, without the feeling of love? Am I a thing? I know that I feel little capacity for love. My capacity for love has been crushed, God knows. There only remains to me a single thread of desire. I *need* for it to be strengthened. For it isn't as you think, that only death matters. To live, a thing you don't know because it's corruptible—to live, rotting away, means a great deal. A dry life: living the essential.

If he gets broken, will you think he has died? No, he's simply left himself. But you do have weaknesses, Sveglia. I heard from your owner that you need a leather case to protect you from the humidity. I also heard, in confidence, that once you actually stopped. The owner didn't get flustered. She just gave you, like, you know, a few little shakes, and you never stopped again. I understand you, I forgive you: you came from Europe, and you need a bit of time to acclimatize yourself, no? Does that mean that you also die, Sveglia? Are you time that stops?

I've even heard Sveglia, over the telephone, go off. It's like inside a person: you wake up from the inside out. It seems that your electronic-God communicates with our electronic-God brain: the sound is mellow, without the least stridency. Sveglia trots on like a white horse, free and without a saddle.

I once heard of a man who owned a Sveglia and to whom Sveglia happened. He was walking along with his ten-year-old son, after dark, and the son said: "Look out, Dad, that's Macumba right there!" The father shrank back—but nonetheless he stepped squarely on the flickering candle, putting it out. Nothing seemed to have happened, which also is just like Sveglia. The man went to bed. When he woke up, he saw that one of his feet was swollen and black. He called for some doctor friends, who couldn't find any sign of a wound: the foot was sound—just black and very swollen, with that kind of swelling that leaves the skin all stretched out. The doctors called in other colleagues. And nine doctors together came to the conclusion that it was gangrene. They would have to amputate the foot. The operation was set for a certain hour the following day. The man fell asleep.

And had a terrible dream. A white horse wanted to attack him, and he fled like a madman. All this was happening in the Campo de Santana. The white horse was beautiful and caparisoned in silver. But there was no way out. The horse grabbed him by the foot, squeezing tight. At this, the man woke up with a shriek. They thought that it was just a case of nerves, they explained that this happens on the eve of an operation, they gave him a sedative, he went back to sleep. When he woke up, he looked immediately at his foot. A shock: the foot was white and back to normal. The nine doctors came and didn't know what to say. They knew nothing of the enigma of Sveglia, against which only a white horse can do battle. There was no longer any reason for the operation. Only he couldn't quite stand on that foot: it had gotten weak. It was the sign of the horse caparisoned in silver, of the extinguished candle, of Sveglia. But Sveglia wished to be victorious, and something happened. The man's wife, in a perfect state of health, at the dinner table, began to feel violent intestinal pains. She left her dinner and went to lie down. The husband, terribly worried, went to see how she was. She was white, bloodless. He took her pulse: nothing. The only sign of life was that her forehead glistened with sweat. The doctor was called and said that perhaps it was a case of catalepsy. The husband had his doubts. He uncovered her belly and made some simple passes over it—as he had himself done when Sveglia had stopped—movements that he didn't know how to explain.

The woman opened her eyes. She was in perfect health. And she's alive to this very day, may God protect her.

This has something to do with Sveglia. I don't know exactly how. But what is, is. And the white horse of the Campo de Santana, a plaza of little birds, pigeons, and coatis? Fully adorned, with silver ornamental gear, with mane aloft and bristling. Running rhythmically against the rhythm of Sveglia. Running without haste.

I am in perfect health, both physical and mental. But one night I was sound asleep and I heard myself cry out loud: "I want to have a child with Sveglia!"

I believe in Sveglia. He doesn't believe in me. He thinks I lie too much. And, in fact, I do. On Earth one lies a great deal.

I went five years without a cold: that's Sveglia. And when I got sick it lasted three days. Then I was left with a dry cough. But the doctor prescribed an antibiotic and cured me. An antibiotic is Sveglia.

This is a report. Sveglia doesn't allow for story or novel or whatever. He just allows transmission. He barely permits me to call this a report. I call it a report on a mystery. And I do everything possible to produce a report as dry as extra-dry champagne. But sometimes—you'll have to excuse me—it gets wet. A dry thing is of sterling silver. Gold, however, is moist. Could I speak of diamonds in relation to Sveglia?

No, he just is. And in reality, Sveglia has no intimate

name: he preserves his anonymity. For that matter, God has no name: he preserves perfect anonymity: there is no tongue that pronounces his true name.

Sveglia is a fool: he acts clandestinely, without thought. I'm now going to say something very serious that will seem like heresy: God is a fool. For he doesn't understand, he doesn't think, he simply is. The truth is that he is of a stupidity that executes itself. And he commits many errors. And he knows that he commits them. All we have to do is look at ourselves, we who are a grave error. All we have to do is see how we organize ourselves, in society and, inwardly, as well. But one error He does not commit: He doesn't die.

Sveglia also doesn't die. I still haven't seen Sveglia, as I said earlier. Maybe seeing him would be moist. I know everything about him. But his owner doesn't want me to see him. She is jealous. Jealousy actually drips when it gets that wet. In fact, our Earth runs the risk of being drenched in sentiment. The rooster is Sveglia. The egg is pure Sveglia. But only the whole egg, complete, white, with a dry shell, perfectly oval. Within is life: moist life. And to eat raw yoke is Sveglia.

Do you want to see who Sveglia is? A soccer game. But Pelé himself is not. Why not? It's impossible to explain. Maybe he hasn't respected anonymity.

A quarrel is Sveglia. I've just had one with the owner of the clock. I said: since you won't let me see Sveglia, at least describe his works to me. Then she became furious—and that is Sveglia—and said that she had tons of problems—to have problems is not Sveglia. Then I tried to calm her down, and everything was O.K. Tomorrow I will not call her. I'll let her rest.

It seems to me I'm going to write about the electronic clock without ever seeing it. It seems that's how it will have to be. It is fated.

I'm getting sleepy. Could such a thing be allowed? I know that to dream is not Sveglia. Numbers are allowed. But six is not. A very few poems are allowed. A novel, however, don't even mention it. Once, for seven days, I had a maid named Severina who had gone hungry as a child. I asked her if she had been sad. She said she was neither happy nor sad: that's just how she was. She was Sveglia. But I was not, and couldn't stand the absence of feeling.

Sweden is Sveglia.

But now I'm going to sleep, although I mustn't dream.

Water, in spite of being wetness *par excellence,* is. To write is. But style isn't. To have breasts is. The male organ is too much so. Kindness isn't. But lack of kindness, selflessness is. Generosity is not the opposite of evil.

Will I be writing moistly? I think so. My surname is. My first name is too sweet, it's for love. To have no secret—and at the same time to remain a mystery—that is Sveglia. In punctuation ellipses are not. If someone understands my unrevealing and precise report, that someone is. It seems that I am not I, so much am I myself. The Sun is, the Moon not. My face is. Probably yours as well. Whiskey is. And, incredible as it seems, Coca-Cola is, while Pepsi-Cola never has been. Am I giving free advertising? That would be wrong, you hear, Coca-Cola?

To be faithful is. The act of love has within it a despair that is.

Now I'm going to tell a story. But first I want to say that the one who told me this story is someone who, in spite of being especially good, is Sveglia.

Now I'm practically dying of exhaustion. Sveglia—if one isn't careful—kills.

The story is the following:

It takes place in a town called Coelho Neto in Guanabara. The woman in this story was very unhappy because she had an ulcer on her leg and the ulcer wouldn't heal. She worked hard and her husband was a mailman. To be a mailman is Sveglia. They had lots of children. Almost nothing to eat. But that mailman took upon himself the responsibility of making his wife happy. To be happy is Sveglia. And the mailman solved the problem. He pointed out to her a neighbor who was barren and suffering greatly because of it. There was no way for her to have a child. He showed his wife how lucky she was to have children. And she became happy, even with so little food. The mailman also pointed out another neighbor who had children, but whose husband drank all the time and beat her and the children. He, on the other hand, didn't drink and never slapped her or the kids. Which made her happy.

Every night they felt sorry for the barren neighbor and the one who got it from her husband. Every night they were very happy. And to be happy is Sveglia. Every night.

I wanted to get to page 9 on my typewriter. The number nine is almost unreachable. The number 13 is God. The typewriter is. The danger of it ceasing to be Sveglia comes from when it is mixed a bit with the feelings of the person who is writing.

One day I got fed up with my Consuls, mentholated and sweet. But Carltons are dry, hard, rough, and share no collusion with the smoker. Since each thing is or is not, it doesn't bother me to be giving Carltons free advertising. But as for Coca-Cola, it's out of the question.

I want to send this report to the magazine *Senhor,* and I want them to pay well for it.

Since you are, decide whether my cook, who cooks well and sings all day long, also is.

I think I will conclude this report so essential for the explanation of energy phenomena in matter. But I don't know what to do. Ah, I'm going to get dressed.

Never again, Sveglia. The sky is very blue. The waves white with sea foam are more than the sea. (I've already taken leave of Sveglia, I just go on talking about him by habit, please have patience.) The smell of the sea mixes masculine and feminine and there is born in the air a child who is.

The owner of the clock told me today that it is he who is her master. She told me that he has little black perforations from which comes a sound soothing as the absence of words, the sound of satin. The inside face is gold-plated. The outer face is silver-plated, almost colorless—like an aircraft in space, flying metal. Waiting is or isn't it? I don't know how to answer because I feel pressed and am unable to decide on this item without getting emotionally involved. I don't like to wait.

A quartet is much more so than a symphony. A flute is. There is an element of horror to a harpsichord: sounds emerge ruffled and brittle. Something from another world.

Sveglia, when, finally, will you leave me in peace? You're not going to pursue me for the rest of my life, transforming it into the clarity of unending insomnia? I really hate you. I wish I could write an account: a short story or a novel or some transmission. What will my next step in literature be? I fear I will never write again. But the truth is that I've had such fears before, and yet I wrote. But what, for God's sake, shall I write? Have I contaminated myself with Sveglia's mathematics and will I only be able to make reports?

And now I shall end this report on a mystery. It so

happens that I'm very tired. Before going out, I'm going to take a bath and perfume myself with my own secret perfume. I'll only say one thing about it: it is earthy and a bit rough, with a hidden sweetness. It is.

Farewell, Sveglia. Farewell for never. A part of me you have already killed. I have died and I am rotting. To die is.

And now—now, farewell.

A MANIFESTO OF THE CITY

Why not try, at this moment that isn't serious, to look
out the window? This is the bridge. This is the river.
There's the Penitentiary. There's the clock. And
Recife. And there, the canal. Where is the stone I feel?
The stone that crushed the city. In the palpable form
of things. For this is a realized city. Its last earthquake
is lost in time. I reach out my hand and without sadness
feel from afar the shape of the stone. Something still
evades the compass rose. Something stiffens in the steel
arrow that points the way to: The Other City.

This moment isn't serious. I take advantage of it and
look out the window. There's a house. I finger your
steps, steps that I have climbed in Recife. Then the
short column. I'm seeing everything extraordinarily
well. Nothing escapes me. A mapped-out city. And
mapped-out with what ingenuity. Stonemasons, car-
penters, engineers, sculptors, artisans—they all took
death into account. My sight is coming clearer by the
minute: this is the house, mine, the bridge, the river, the
Penitentiary, the square blocks of buildings, the stair-
way empty of myself, the stone.

But look how a Horse appears. Behold, a horse with
four legs and hooves hard as stone, a strong neck, and
the head of a Horse. Behold a horse!

If you were a word echoing on the hard ground, what

would you mean? How hollow this heart in the breast of the city! I search, I search. House, sidewalks, steps, monument, lamppost, your industriousness.

From the highest rampart—I look out. I search. On the highest rampart I receive no signal. From here I don't see, for your clarity is impenetrable. From here I don't see, but I sense that something is written in charcoal on a wall. On a wall in this city.

THE WHITE ROSE

Lofty petal: epitome of surface. Cathedral of glass, surface of all surfaces, unreachable by voice. From your stalk, two voices join with a third and a fifth and a ninth—wise children open mouths in the morning and intone the spirit, spirit, surface, spirit, untouchable surface of a rose.

I reach out my left hand, which is the weaker, the dark hand, and I quickly draw it back, smiling with embarrassment. I cannot touch you. My rough-grained spirit wishes to sing your new understanding of ice and of glory.

I try to remember memory, to understand you as one sees the dawn, a chair, another flower. Do not fear, I don't want to possess you. I raise myself toward your surface, which now is perfume.

I raise myself till I reach my own seeming. I grow pale in this frightened fine region, I almost reach your divine surface . . .

In my ridiculous fall, I break an angel's wings. I do not bow my snarling head: I want at least to suffer your victory with the angelic suffering of your harmony, your joy. But my heart aches, coarse as with love for a man.

And from hands so very large flies the word, ashamed.

THE CONJURATIONS OF DONA FROZINA

"Even with these withered old bills . . ."

That's what the widow Dona Frozina says of her pension. But it's enough so she can buy Leite de Rosas and actually bathe in the milky liquid. They say her skin is a marvel. She's used the same product since her early teens, and she smells of mother.

She's very religious and practically lives in churches. All this, smelling of Leite de Rosas. Like a girl. She became a widow at the age of twenty-nine. And from then till now—nothing to do with men. An old-fashioned widow. Austere. No dipping necklines and always in long sleeves.

"Dona Frozina, how have you managed without a man?" I would like to ask.

The answer would be:

"Conjurations," my child, "conjurations."

They say of her: lots of youngsters don't have the spirit she has. She's in her seventies, her Excellency Madame Dona Frozina. She's a good mother-in-law and a splendid grandmother. A good dam she was as well. And she kept on producing. If there's someone I'd like to have a talk with, it's Dona Frozina.

"Dona Frozina, do you have something in common with Dona Flor and her three husbands?"

"What are you saying, my dear, but how very sinful! I am a virgin-widow, my child."

Her husband's name was Epaminondas, but they called him Moço, "Buster."

Look, Dona Frozina, there are worse names than yours. There's someone named Flor de Lis—but since they found it a crummy name, they gave her a nickname that was even worse: Dody. Practically Doody. And the countries that they name their children: Brazil, Argentina, Colombia, Belgium, and France? You escaped being a country. You and your conjurations. "There's not much in it," she says, "but it's fun."

Fun in what way, madam? Haven't you, after all, known suffering? Have you been dodging suffering all your life? Yes, m'am, with my conjurations I've escaped it.

Dona Frozina doesn't drink Coca-Cola. She thinks it's too modern.

"But everyone drinks it!"

"Well, I don't, God forbid! It's like some tapeworm medicine. God save and protect me."

But if she thinks it tastes like medicine, that's because she's already tried it.

Dona Frozina uses the name of the Lord more than she should. One shouldn't take God's name in vain. But the commandment doesn't apply to her.

And she clings to the saints. The saints must be sick of her, she's abused them so. As for "Our Lady," don't even mention it; the mother of Jesus has no peace. In fact, since she's from the north, she lives with "Virgin Marys" coming from her mouth at every little fright. And the little frights of the ingenuous widow are many.

Dona Frozina would always say her prayers at night. She would make a special invocation to each saint. Then disaster struck: one night, she fell asleep in the middle.

"Dona Frozina, what a terrible thing, to doze off in the middle of a prayer, leaving the saints to fend for themselves."

She answered with a dismissive wave of the hand:

"Ah, my child, let each look after his own."

She had a most strange dream: she dreamed that she saw the Christ of Corcovado—but what had become of his wide-spread arms? Now they were tightly crossed, and Christ with a disgusted scowl, as if to say: you folks take care of yourselves, I've had it. It was a sin, that dream.

Dona Frozina, enough of your conjurations. Stick to your Leite de Rosas and your "io me ne vado." (Is that what you say in Italian when you want to leave?)

Dona Frozina, most excellent lady, the one who's had it with you is me. Farewell, then. I've dozed off in the middle of a prayer.

P.S. Look up the meaning of conjurations in the dictionary. But I'll do it for you: conjuration—the casting of magical spells, the invocation of spirits; an incantation; a trick. (From the Shorter Brazilian Dictionary of the Portuguese Language).

One detail before I stop:

Dona Frozina, when she was little, out in Sergipe, ate squatting behind the kitchen door. No one knows why.

THAT'S WHERE I'M GOING

Beyond the ear there is a sound, at the farthest reaches of sight a shape, at fingertip's end an object—and that's where I'm going.

At the tip of the pencil the line.

Where a thought expires is an idea, behind the last breath of joy another joy, at the point of a sword magic—that's where I'm going.

At the tip of one's toes the leap.

It's like the story of someone who went off and didn't return—that's where I'm going.

Or won't I go? Yes, I'll go. And I'll come back to see how things are. Whether they are still magical. Reality? I await you. That's where I'm going.

At the tip of a word is a word. I want to use the word "foregathering," but I don't know when or where to use it. At the edge of the foregathering is the family. At the edge of the family is me. At my own edge is me. It is to myself that I'm going. And I leave myself in order to see. To see what? To see what there is. After death it's to reality I'll go. For the time being it's a dream. A fateful dream. But afterward—afterward everything is real. And the free soul looks for a corner in which to settle. I am an I that I announce. I don't know what I'm talking about. I'm talking about nothing. I am nothing. After death I will grow and scatter myself, and someone will say my name with love.

It is to my poor name that I'm going.

And from there I will return to call the name of my loved one and my children. They will answer me. Finally I will have an answer. What answer? That of love. Love: I love you so much. I love love. Love is red. Jealousy is green. My eyes are green. But their green is so dark that in a photograph they come out black. My secret is that I have green eyes and nobody knows.

At my outer reaches it is still I. I, imploring, I, the one who needs, the one who begs, the one who cries, the one who grieves. But the one who sings. The one who says words. Words to the wind? What does it matter, the winds bring them back again, and I repossess them.

I at the edge of the wind. The wuthering heights call me. I go, witch that I am. And I transmute myself.

Oh dog, where has your soul gone to? Is it at the edge of your body? I am at the edge of my body. And I slowly fade away.

What am I saying? I'm saying love. And at the edge of love—there we stand.

THE DEAD MAN IN THE SEA
AT URCA

I was at the apartment of Dona Lourdes, my seamstress, trying on a new dress designed by Olly—and Dona Lourdes said: "A man drowned in the sea, look at the firemen." I looked and only saw the sea, which must have been very salty; blue sea, white houses. And the dead man?

The dead man pickled in brine. I don't want to die! I screamed to myself, silent within my dress. The dress is yellow and blue. And I? Dying of heat, not dying of a blue sea.

I'll tell you a secret: my dress is beautiful, and I don't want to die. On Friday the dress will be at home, and on Saturday I'll wear it. Without death, just blue sea. Do yellow clouds exist? Golden ones do. I have no story. Does the dead man? He does: he went to take a swim in the sea at Urca, the fool, and he died—who told him to go? I'm careful when I bathe in the sea, I'm no fool, and I only go to Urca to try on a new dress. And three blouses. S. went with me. She is most particular at a fitting. And the dead man? Particularly dead?

I'll tell you a story: once upon a time there was a young fellow who liked to swim in the sea. So, one Wednesday morning he went to Urca. I don't go to Urca, to the rocks of Urca, because it's full of rats. But the young man didn't pay any attention to the rats. Nor

148

did the rats pay any attention to him. Urca's cluster of
white houses. That he noticed. And then there was a
woman trying on a dress, who arrived too late: the
young man was already dead. Briny. Were there pira-
nhas in the sea? I pretended not to understand. I don't,
in fact, understand death. A boy, dead?

Dead like the fool he was. One should only go to Urca
to try on a gay dress. The woman, who is me, only
wants gaiety. But I bow down before death. That will
come, will come, will come. When? Ah, that's just it, it
can come at any moment. But I, who was trying on a
dress in the heat of the morning, asked God for a sign.
And I felt something so intense, an overwhelming scent
of roses. So, I had my proof, in two tests: of God and
of my dress.

One should only die a natural death, never in an
accident, never drowned in the sea. I beg protection for
my own, who are many. And the protection, I am sure,
will come.

But what of the young man? And his story? He might
have been a student. I will never know. I simply stood
staring out at the sea and the cluster of houses. Dona
Lourdes, imperturbable, asked if she should take it in
at the waist a bit more. I said yes, a waistline is there
to be seen tight. But I was in shock. In shock in my
beautiful new dress.

SILENCE

So vast, the silence of the night on the mountain. So desolate. One tries in vain to work so as not to hear it, to think rapidly so as to mask it. Or to make up a program, a fragile point that barely links us to a suddenly improbable tomorrow. How to pass beyond this peace that lies in wait for us. A silence so great that hopelessness is shamed. Mountains so high that hopelessness is shamed. Ears perk, one's head tilts, the whole body listens: not a sound. Not a single rooster. How to come within reach of this deep meditation of silence. This silence with no memory of words. If you are death, how to reach you.

It is a silence that doesn't sleep. It is awake: immobile, but awake; and without ghosts. It is awful—without a single ghost. Useless, the wish to populate it with the possibility of a door creaking open, of a curtain drawing back and saying something. It is empty and without promise. If at least there were a wind. Wind is wrath, wrath is life. Or if there were snow. Which is mute, but leaves traces—everything turns white, children laugh, steps squeak and leave their mark. There is a continuity that is life. But this silence leaves no evidence behind. One cannot speak of silence as one does of snow. One cannot say to anyone as one would of the snow: did you feel the silence of the night? Whoever noticed isn't saying.

Night falls with those little joys of someone turning on the lights with that tiredness that so justifies the day. The children of Berne fall asleep, the last doors are closed. The streets glisten, in their cobblestones, glisten, already empty. And, finally, the most distant lights go out.

But this first silence isn't yet silence. Let us wait, for the leaves of the trees will still settle themselves more comfortably, and some belated footsteps on the stairs may still awaken hope.

But there comes a moment when, from the quiet body and from the earth to the moon above, an attentive spirit rises. And then, then, silence appears.

The heart pounds in recognition.

One can quickly think of the day that has just passed. Or of friends who have passed away and are lost forever. But these evasions are useless: the silence is there. Even the worst suffering, that of lost friendship, is merely an escape. For if in the beginning the silence seems to be awaiting a response—how we burn to be called to answer—soon enough it becomes clear that it demands nothing of you, only perhaps your silence. How many hours are lost in the darkness, imagining that the silence is judging you—how we wait in vain to be judged by God. Justifications, tragically forged justifications, rise up, excuses humble to the point of indignity. So soothing it is for a human being finally to expose his unworthiness and be pardoned simply on the grounds that he is a human being, humiliated from birth.

Until it becomes clear—it doesn't even want your degradation. It is silence.

One can also try to trick it. To let the bedside book fall to the floor, as if by chance. But, oh horror—the book falls into silence and is lost in its mute and motionless abyss. And what if a crazed bird were to sing? A futile hope. The song would merely float across the silence like a gentle flute.

So, if you have courage, you give up struggling. You enter it, go with it, we the only ghosts of this night in Berne. Just enter it. Don't wait for the rest of darkness beyond it, just wait for it itself. It will be as if we are on a ship so incredibly immense that we don't even know we are on a ship. And it will sail so broadly that we won't know that we are moving. A man can do no more. To live on the edge of death and of the stars is a vibration too tense for our veins to endure. There isn't even the child of a star and a woman as a compassionate intermediary. The heart must present itself alone before nothingness, and alone it must beat loud in the darkness. In your ears, you only hear your own heart. When it appears completely naked, that's not communication, it's submission. For we were made for nothing if not the little silence.

If you do not have courage, then do not enter. Then wait for the rest of darkness, beyond silence, with only your feet wet from the foam of something that overflows from within us. Wait. Each inexplicable to the other. Each next to the other, two things unseen in the dark. Wait then. Not for the end of silence, but the blessed aid of a third element, the light of dawn.

Afterward, you will never forget. Even to flee to another city is pointless. For just when you least expect it, you may recognize it—suddenly! While crossing the street in the middle of the blaring horns. Between one phantasmagoric burst of laughter and another. After a word is said. Sometimes in the very heart of a word. One listens startled, one stares into space—there it is! And this time it *is* a ghost.

AN EMPTYING

It isn't that we had been friends for a long time. We only got to know each other in our last year at school. But from that time on, we could be found together at all hours. Both of us had been in need of a friend for so long that there was nothing we wouldn't tell each other. Our friendship reached a point where we couldn't keep a single thought to ourselves: we would quickly call each other and agree to meet right away. After our talk, we would feel as happy as if we had given ourselves a present. This state of continual communication reached such a level of exaltation that, on days when we had nothing to tell each other, we would anxiously search for some topic to discuss. Only the subject had to be serious, for each of us was bursting with the vehemence of a sincerity experienced for the first time.

Yet already back then, the first signs of trouble between us had begun to appear. Sometimes one of us would call, we would meet, and we would have nothing to say to one another. We were very young, and we didn't know how to remain silent. At first, when we began to run out of things to say, we tried talking about people. But we really knew that we were already adulterating the nucleus of our friendship. To try to speak of our respective girlfriends was also out of the question, since a man never spoke of his loves. We tried remaining silent—but we would feel uneasy shortly after having parted.

My loneliness on returning from such a meeting was vast and sterile. I ended up reading books just to be able to talk about them. But a real friendship yearns for the purest sincerity. In searching for it, I began to feel empty. Each time we met, our disappointment grew. My genuine poverty began to reveal itself, bit by bit. He also, I knew, had arrived at an impasse within himself.

It was then, my family having moved to São Paulo, and he living alone, since his family was from Piauí, it was then that I invited him to live in our apartment, which had remained in my charge. What an uproar in my soul. Radiant, we arranged our books and records, preparing the perfect environment for friendship. When everything was ready, there we were, at loose ends, silent, filled only with friendship.

How we wished to save each other! Friendship is the stuff of salvation.

But all problems had already been touched upon, all possibilities considered. We had nothing but the thing which we had so thirsted after until then and had finally found: a real friendship. The only way, we knew, and with what bitterness we knew it, to escape from the loneliness of a spirit locked in its body.

But how artificial our friendship was turning out to be. As if we were trying to stretch into a long speech a truism for which a single word would suffice. Our friendship was as indissoluble as the sum of two numbers: it is pointless to want to expand beyond a moment the certainty that two plus three equals five.

We tried to throw some wild parties in the apartment, but it wasn't only the complaints of the neighbors—it just didn't work out.

If at least we could have done each other favors. But there were no opportunities, nor did we believe in the proofs of a friendship that needed them. The most we could do was what we were doing: just know that we were friends. Which was not enough to fill our days, especially during the long vacation.

The beginning of our true suffering dates from that vacation time.

He, to whom I could give nothing but my sincerity, he came to be a daily reminder of my poverty. Worst of all, the loneliness of being next to each other, listening to music or reading, was much greater than when we had been alone. And worse than that, it was uncomfortable. There was no peace. Later, as we each would go to our own room, relieved, we wouldn't even look at one another.

It is true that there was a pause in the course of events, a truce that gave us more hope than it should have. It was when my friend had a minor problem with City Hall. Not that it was serious, but we turned it to our best advantage. For by then we had fallen into the habit of doing each other favors. I went in great excitement to the offices of family acquaintances, arranging influential support for my friend. And when the time came for getting documents stamped, I ran all over town—I can say, in all truthfulness, that nothing was notarized except through my hands.

During this period, we would meet at home at night, exhausted and excited: we spoke of the day's exploits and planned the next attacks. We didn't look deeply into what was happening, it was enough that all of this had the seal of friendship. I thought I understood why sweethearts give each other presents, why the husband strives to provide his wife with all the comforts, why she so diligently prepares the food, why mothers are overcareful with their children. It was, furthermore, in this period that, with a certain sacrifice, I gave a small golden brooch to the one who today is my wife. Only much later would I understand that to be is also to give.

When the problem with City Hall was resolved— may it be said, in passing, with our victory—we remained side by side, unable to find the word that yields up the soul. That yields up the soul? But after all, who would want to yield up their soul? Just imagine!

In the end, what did we want? Nothing. We were worn out and disillusioned.

Using a vacation with my parents as an excuse, we separated. As a matter of fact, he himself was going to Piauí. An emotional handshake was our good-by at the airport. We knew that we would never see each other again, unless by chance. What's more, that we wouldn't want to see each other again. And we also knew that we were friends. Real friends.

A FULL AFTERNOON

The tamarin is as small as a rat and the same color.

The woman, after sitting down in the bus and casting a peaceful, proprietary glance along the seats, swallowed a scream: next to her, in the hands of a fat man, was something which looked like a restless rat and which, in reality, was a most lively tamarin. The first moments of woman versus monkey were spent in her trying to feel that it wasn't a question of a rat in disguise.

When this was accomplished, delicious and intense moments began: the observation of the creature. The whole bus, for that matter, did nothing else.

But it was the woman's privilege to be right next to the main character. From where she was, for example, she could see the tininess that is a tamarin's tongue: the slash of a red pencil.

And there were teeth, too: you could almost count about a thousand teeth within the slash of the mouth, and each sliver smaller than the next, and whiter. The monkey didn't shut its mouth for a moment.

Its eyes, rounded and hyperthyroid, combined with a slight prognathism of the lower jaw—and this mixture gave him a strangely impudent expression, forming the half-proffered face of a street urchin, one of those who always have colds and sniffle while sucking on candy.

When the monkey jumped onto the woman's lap, she repressed a *frisson* and the shy pleasure of one who is chosen.

But the passengers looked at her with sympathy, approving of what was happening, and, blushing a bit, she accepted her role as timid favorite. She didn't pet him because she didn't know if this would be the right thing to do.

As a matter of fact, the creature didn't suffer from lack of affection. Actually, his owner, the fat man, felt a solid, severe love for him, that of a father for a son, of a master for his wife. He was a man who, without a smile, possessed the proverbial heart of gold. The expression of his face was even tragic, as if he had a mission in life. A mission of love? The monkey was his faithful dog.

The bus, as if fluttering with banners, advanced through the breeze. The monkey ate a cookie. The monkey scratched rapidly at its round ear with one of its thin hind legs. The monkey shrieked. It clung to the window and took quick peeks out—startling faces in passing buses which showed shock and hadn't the time to verify whether they had really seen what they had seen.

Meanwhile, near the woman, one woman told another that she had a cat. Whoever loved something told about it.

It was in this happy family atmosphere that a truck tried to pass the bus, and there was a near-fatal collision. Screams. Everyone quickly jumped out. The woman, late for an appointment, took a taxi.

Only in the taxi did she again remember the monkey.

And she lamented with a mirthless smile—since the days went by so full of news in the papers and with so little for her—that events had been distributed so badly that a monkey and a near disaster should occur at the same time.

"I'll bet," she thought, "that nothing else happens to me for a long time, I'll bet that now I'm in for some lean times." Which, for her, was normally the case.

But that same day other things happened. All kinds of things, including some in the category of declarable assets. Only they weren't communicable. This woman was, as a matter of fact, rather silent with herself and didn't really understand herself very well.

But that's how it is. And a monkey has never been heard of who failed to be born, live, and die—just because he didn't understand himself or wasn't understood.

In any case, it was an afternoon of fluttering banners.

SUCH GENTLENESS

A dark hour, perhaps the darkest, in broad day, preceded this thing I don't even want to try to define. In the middle of the day it is night, and this thing I still don't want to define is a peaceful light inside me, you might call it gladness, gentle gladness. I am a bit disoriented as if the heart had been taken out of me, and in its place there now were a sudden absence, an absence, almost palpable, of what before had been an organ bathed in a darkness of pain. I feel nothing. But it is the opposite of a stupor. It is a lighter, more silent way of living.

But I am also uneasy. I was all prepared to console myself in my anguish and pain. But how can I accommodate myself to this simple and peaceful gladness. It's that I'm not used to not needing to console myself. The word console came without my sensing it, and I didn't even notice, and when I went in search of it, it had already transformed itself into flesh and spirit, it no longer existed as a thought.

I go, then, to the window; it is raining heavily. By habit I search in the rain for what at another time would serve to console me. But I have no grief to console.

Ah, I know. I am now searching in the rain for a joy so great that it would become razor sharp, a joy which would put me in touch with an intensity resembling the intensity of pain. But the search is useless. I am at the window, and only this happens: I see the rain with benevolent eyes, and the rain sees me, and all is in harmony. We are both busy flowing. How long will my condition last? I notice that, with this question, I finger my pulse to feel where the painful throbbing of before should be. And I see that there is no painful throbbing.

Only this: it rains, and I watch the rain. What simplicity. I never thought that the world and I would reach this point. The rain falls, not because it needs me, and I look at the rain, not because I need it. But we are as united as the water of the rain is to the rain. And I am not giving thanks for anything. If shortly after birth I hadn't taken, involuntarily, by compulsion, the road I took—I would have always been what in fact I really am: a country girl in a field where it is raining. Not even thanking God or nature. The rain too expresses no gratitude. I am not a thing that is thankful for having been transformed into something else. I am a woman, I am a person, I am an attention. I am a body looking out through the window. Just as the rain is not grateful for not being a stone. It is rain. Perhaps it is this that might be called being alive. No more than this, but this: alive. And alive just through gentle gladness.

WATERS OF THE SEA

There it is, the sea, the most incomprehensible of non-human existences. And here is the woman, standing on the beach, the most incomprehensible of living beings. As the human being one day asked itself a question about itself, it became the most incomprehensible of living beings. She and the sea.

Their mysteries can only meet if one surrenders to the other: the surrender of two unknowable worlds, made with the confidence with which two understandings give themselves up.

She looks at the sea, that is what she can do. Only the line of the horizon limits it for her, that is to say, only her human incapacity to see the curvature of the earth.

It is six in the morning. There's just a dog loose on the beach, a black dog, hesitant. Why is it that a dog is so free? Because it is the living mystery that doesn't question itself. The woman pauses, for she is about to enter.

Her body consoles itself with its own smallness in relation to the vastness of the sea, for it is the smallness of the body that allows it to keep itself warm, and it is this smallness that makes her a poor and free person, with her share of the freeness of a dog on the sand. That body will enter into the unending coldness that without anger roars in the silence of six A.M. The woman

162

doesn't understand: but she rises to her courage. With the beach empty at that hour of the morning, she doesn't have the example of other humans who transform entering the sea into a simple, frivolous game of life. She is alone. The salt sea is not alone, for it is salty and immense, a thing achieved. At that hour she knows herself even less than she knows the sea. Her courage is that of not knowing oneself, yet going ahead. It is fatal not to know oneself, and not to know oneself demands courage.

And now she enters. The briny water is of a coldness that sends her legs into a ritual shiver. But a fatal joy— joy is fatal—has already enveloped her, although it doesn't occur to her to smile. On the contrary, she is very serious. The intoxicating odor of the briny sea awakens her from centuries of slumber. And now she is alert, even without thinking. The woman is now firm, fine, keen-edged—and she opens a path in the iciness which, liquid, resists her and yet allows her to enter, as in love, where resistance can be a request.

Her slow pace builds her secret courage. And, suddenly, she lets herself be covered by the first wave. The salt, the iodine, all liquid, leave her for a moment blind, dripping—and she stands, stunned, fertilized.

Now the cold turns frigid. Advancing, she cuts open the sea. And now she no longer needs courage, now she is already ancient in the ritual. She lowers her head into the sparkle of the sea, and draws forth masses of hair dripping all over her salty, burning eyes. She plays with her hand in the water, leisurely, her hair in the sun almost immediately stiffening with salt. Hands cupped, she does what she has always done in the sea, and with the pride of those who will never explain, not even to themselves: from her cupped hands filled with water, she drinks, in great, wonderful gulps.

And it was this that she had been missing: the sea inside, like the thick fluid of a man. Now she is completely equal to herself. The nourished throat tightens from the salt, her eyes turn red from the salt dried by the sun, the gentle waves slap against her and fall back, for she is a solid barrier.

She dives again, again she drinks, more water, but no longer ravenous, for she needs no more. She is the lover who knows that she will have it all again. The sun breaks through, and she shivers as it dries her, and then she dives again; she is less and less greedy, less keen-edged. Now she knows what she wants. She wants to stand still in the sea. So she does. As against the hull of a ship, the water beats, withdraws, beats. Nothing is transmitted. Communication is not necessary.

Later she walks through the water back to the beach. She is not walking upon the waters—ah, never would she do that, for thousands of years ago they had already walked upon the waters—but no one will take this from her: walking through the water. At moments the sea gathers to oppose her, pulling her back by force, but then the prow of the woman advances, a little harder, a little rougher.

And now she steps out on the sand. She knows that she is glistening with water, salt, and sun. Even if she forgets it a few minutes from now, she will never lose all this. And she knows in some obscure way that her dripping hair is that of a castaway. For she knows—she knows that she has passed through danger. Danger as ancient as the human race.

SOULSTORM

Ah, had I but known, I wouldn't have come into this world, ah, had I but known, I wouldn't have come into this world. Madness is neighbor to the cruelest prudence. I swallow madness because it calmly leads me to hallucinations. Jack and Jill went up the hill to fetch a pail of water, Jack fell down, Jill kissed his crown, and they lived happy-unhappy ever after. The chair is an object to me. It is useless while I look at it. Tell me, please, what time it is, so I'll know I'm alive at that time. Creativity is unleashed by a germ and I don't have that germ today, but I do have an incipient madness which in itself is a valid creation. I have nothing more to do with the validity of things. I am free or lost. I'm going to tell you a secret: life is lethal. We maintain the secret in utter silence, each of us, as we face ourselves, because to do so is convenient and doing otherwise would make each moment lethal. The object chair has always interested me. I look at this one, which is old, bought at an antique shop, an Empire chair; one couldn't imagine a greater simplicity of line contrasting with the seat of red felt. I love objects in proportion to how little they love me. But if I don't understand what I am writing, the fault isn't mine. I have to speak, for speaking saves me. But I don't have a single word to say. I am gagged by words already spoken. What does one person say to another? How about "how's it going?" If the madness of honesty worked, what would people say to one another? The worst of it is what a person would say to himself, yet that would be his salvation, even if honesty is determined on a conscious level while the terror of honesty comes from the part it plays in the vast unconscious that links me to the world and to the creative unconscious of the world. Today is a day for a starry sky, at least so promises this sad afternoon that a human word could save.

I open my eyes wide, but it does no good: I merely see. But the secret, that I neither see nor feel. The record player is broken, and to live without music is to betray the human condition, which is surrounded by music. Besides, music is an abstraction of thought, I'm speaking of Bach, Vivaldi, Handel. I can only write if I am free, uncensored, otherwise I succumb. I look at the Empire chair, and this time it is as if it too had looked and seen me. The future is mine as long as I live. In the future there will be more time to live and, higgledy-piggledy, to write. In the future one will say: had I but known, I wouldn't have come into this world. Marli de Oliveira, I don't write to you because I only know how to be intimate. In fact, all I can do, whatever the circumstances, is be intimate: that's why I'm even more silent. Everything that never got done, will it one day get done? The future of technology threatens to destroy all that is human in man, but technology does not touch madness; and it is there that the human in man takes refuge. I see the flowers in the vase: they are wildflowers, born without having been planted, they are beautiful and yellow. But my cook says: what ugly flowers. Just because it is difficult to understand and love what is spontaneous and Franciscan. To understand the difficult is no advantage, but to love what is easy to love is a great step upward on the human ladder. How many lies I am forced to tell. But with myself I don't want to be forced to lie. Otherwise what remains to me? Truth is the final residue of all things, and in my unconscious is the same truth as that of the world. The Moon, as Paul Eluard would say, is *éclatante de silence*. I don't know if the Moon will show at all today, since it is already late and I don't see it anywhere in the sky. Once I looked up at the night sky, circumscribing it with my head tilted back, and I became dizzy from the many stars that appear in the country, for the country sky is clear. There is no logic, if one were to think a bit about it, in the perfectly balanced illogicity of nature. Nor in that of human nature either. What would the world be like, the cosmos, if man did not exist? If I could always write as I am writing now, I would be in the midst of a *tempestade de cérebro,* a "brainstorm." Who might have invented the chair? Someone who loved himself. He therefore invented a greater comfort for his body. Then centuries passed and no one really paid attention anymore to a chair, for using it is simply automatic. You have to have courage to stir up a brain-storm: you never know what may come to frighten us. The sacred monster died: in its place a solitary girl was born. I understand, of course, that I will have to stop, not for lack of words, but because such things, and above all those things I've only thought and not written down, usually don't make it into print.

LIFE *AU NATUREL*

Well, in Rio there was a house with a fireplace. And when she saw that besides the cold, rain came down on the trees, she couldn't believe that so much had been given her. The harmony of the world with what she hadn't even known she needed, like someone starving. It rained and rained. The fire winks at her and at the man. He, the man, busies himself with what she doesn't even thank him for; he tends the fire in the fireplace, which for him is no less than his duty by birth. And she—who is always restless, a doer of things, a dabbler in the unusual—well, she doesn't even remember to tend the fire: it isn't her role, since she has her man for that. Not being a damsel, let the man then do his duty! The most she does is sometimes spur him on: "That log," she tells him, "it hasn't caught yet." And he, an instant before she finishes the sentence that would enlighten him, he, on his own, has already noticed the log, his own man that he is, and is already poking it. Not by her command, she who is the woman of a man and would lose her status if she gave him orders. His other hand, the free one, is within her reach. She knows and doesn't take it. She longs for his hand, she knows she wants it, and she doesn't take it. She has exactly what she needs: she could have it.

Ah, and to think that it will end, that in itself it

cannot last. No, she isn't referring to the fire, she is thinking of what she feels. What one feels never lasts, what one feels always ends, and can never again return. She harries the moment, she devours its fire, and the fire sweetly burns, burns, and blazes. So, she who knows that everything will end takes the man's free hand, and taking it in hers sweetly burns, burns, and blazes.

AFTERWORD

"We are all failures," Lispector exclaims in her story "The Man Who Appeared." "Success is a lie." These are rather comforting words to the translator, who is condemned, almost by definition, to fail. Because sound and sense, form and content, are so intimately meshed in serious writing, the translator can only hope for a noble effort, an honorable defeat. Translation is clearly postlapsarian. It *must* be imperfect.

All the more so with a flagrantly idiosyncratic genius like Clarice Lispector, whose distaste for conventions, rules, and orderly classification permeates her work. If the translator produces a smooth, accessible English version, he has been unfaithful to the original. If he strives to be true, he will be accused of awkwardness. Caught in this dilemma, I have perhaps leaned a bit toward readability. However, in the daemonic nightmare "Where You Were at Night," I retained all the disconcerting fragmentation and disjointedness of the original, presuming the structure itself to be part of the nightmare.

Beyond the notorious difficulty of her style lies the problem of voice or tone, and finally the question of her artistic-spiritual stance. What is it that unites these twenty-nine pieces of prose? Genre won't help: there are parables, fairy tales, nightmares, sketches, prose-poems, meditations, interior monologues, newspaper *cronicas.* Lispector, suspicious of all categories, wouldn't call most of these pieces stories. Nor does she allow *herself* to be pinned down. She is irritated when critics link her to Sartre or other "influences." She considers herself *sui generis,* an *isolado,* and, indeed, her choppy brushstrokes often seem those of an alien. Nevertheless, by focusing on her tone of voice, we can identify a deeply human force that flows throughout her art.

A hint from Lispector may help. In her short piece "That's Where I'm Going," she ends with the words: "What am I saying? I am saying love. And at the edge of love—there we stand." This conclusion reveals what I take to be the essence of Lispector's greatness. Like Chekhov, whom she greatly admired, Lispector has the precious gift of evoking love for ordinary people through an understated, often casual or matter-of-fact tone that feigns indifference, while stirring human sympathies in the reader. She gives us brusque encounters with average folk to whom nothing ever happens, but through the very dryness of her style draws forth our compassion. It is as if the starkness of presentation leaves her simple, limited, unfulfilled human creatures more sharply in relief, as if the style, by echoing the "objective" indifference of a vast universe, calls all the more deeply for our compassion. That her own compassion is engaged can be gathered from what she says in an earlier work, *The Foreign Legion* (1964): "I have a deep affection for things that are incomplete or badly finished, for things that awkwardly try to take flight only to end up clumsily on the ground." Surely these words can apply to many of the lives etched rapidly and painfully in this book.

Wary of the rational, Lispector has little faith in words. However, she does believe that by indirection words can achieve something. Again in *The Foreign Legion* she writes:

> Since one feels obliged to write, let it be without obscuring the space between the lines with words. . . . The word fishes for something that is not a word. And when that non-word takes the bait, something has been written. Once the space between the lines has been fished, the word can be thrown away with relief.

Apparently, then, Lispector feels that a human truth that cannot be stated can be conveyed by *non-words*, between the lines. While the written line presents daily life or struggles in vain for truth through reason, the real discovery, love, rises like a great old bass through the empty spaces.

Clarice Lispector is fundamentally a poet. Relying heavily on intuition, she mixes subjectivity and objectivity, spontaneity and detachment, self-indulgence and irony, to draw us all together, readers, characters, and writer: faced with our smallness and our mortality, we *must* love one another. And thanks to Clarice Lispector's skill and humanity, we do.

Since this adventure began fifteen years ago, I have many people to thank. First of all, Irene Ribarolli Pereira da Silva, who, in giving me a huge package of books as my Brazilian going-away present, bestowed on me copies of the two Lispector collections that make up this volume. Then there is my mother, Isabella Yanovsky, whose enthusiasm for Lispector fueled an unrelenting insistence that I complete this task, despite my prolonged bouts with linguistic despair. In addition to spurring me on whenever I dropped in my tracks, she also read with great care the bulk of my manuscript and made numerous useful suggestions. Then there are the Brazilians who kindly helped me in my struggle with Lispector's stylistic peculiarities. Though I must apologize to some whose names have been swallowed by time, the principal actors, scattered across the country and the years, are Cristina Guimarães in New York City, Luiz Valente at Brown University, Neise Turchin in Palo Alto, and Mrs. Douglas Graham of Columbus, Ohio. In addition, my good friend, the ideal translator's informant, Clara Pires, gave a meticulous reading to my entire manuscript. Claire Varin, a Quebecoise authority on Lispector, allowed me a full day of her time and passed on to me an intensely powerful impression of Lispector's character. Professor Reed Anderson of Miami University in Ohio was most encouraging early on, and his commentaries helped influence my final text. I would also like to thank his colleagues Alice Fox, Nathaniel Wing, and Peter Williams, all of whom were connected with this book when it was originally being prepared for the Miami University/Ohio State University Joint Imprint Press. Closer to home, I would like to thank Peter Glassgold at New Directions for solid support, good-humored editing, and his overall role in promoting the art of translation. In addition to the above individuals, I must thank the Research Foundations of Denison University and the State University of New York at Plattsburgh for helping to support this project. And finally, I am most pleased to acknowledge the role of Columbia University's Translation Center, which honored me with the

Van de Bovenkamp-Armand G. Erpf International Award for the translations which are now appearing in this book.

ALEXIS LEVITIN

New Directions Paperbooks – A Partial Listing

For complete listing request free catalog from
New Directions, 80 Eighth Avenue, New York 10011
† Bilingual

The Smile at the Foot of the Ladder. NDP386.
  Stand Still Like the Hummingbird. NDP236.
  The Time of the Assassins. NDP115.
Y. Mishima, Confessions of a Mask. NDP253.
  Death in Midsummer. NDP215.
Frédéric Mistral, The Memoirs. NDP632.
Eugenio Montale, It Depends.† NDP507.
  New Poems. NDP410.
  Selected Poems.† NDP193.
Paul Morand, Fancy Goods/Open All Night.
  NDP567.
Vladimir Nabokov, Nikolai Gogol. NDP78.
  Laughter in the Dark. NDP470.
  The Real Life of Sebastian Knight. NDP432.
P. Neruda, The Captain's Verses.† NDP345.
  Residence on Earth.† NDP340.
New Directions in Prose & Poetry (Anthology).
  Available from #17 forward to #52.
Robert Nichols, Arrival. NDP437.
  Exile. NDP485. Garh City. NDP450.
  Harditts in Sawna. NDP470.
Charles Olson, Selected Writings. NDP231.
Toby Olson, The Life of Jesus. NDP417.
  Seaview. NDP532.
George Oppen, Collected Poems. NDP418.
István Örkeny, The Flower Show /
  The Toth Family. NDP536.
Wilfred Owen, Collected Poems. NDP210.
José Emilio Pacheco, Battles in the Desert, NDP637.
  Selected Poems.† NDP638.
Nicanor Parra, Antipoems: New & Selected. NDP603.
Boris Pasternak, Safe Conduct. NDP77.
Kenneth Patchen, Aflame and Afun. NDP292.
  Because It Is. NDP83.
  Collected Poems. NDP284.
  Hallelujah Anyway. NDP219.
  Selected Poems. NDP160.
Octavio Paz, Configurations.† NDP303.
  A Draft of Shadows.† NDP489.
  Eagle or Sun?† NDP422.
  Selected Poems. NDP574.
  A Tree Within,† NDP661.
St. John Perse. Selected Poems.† NDP545.
J. A. Porter, Eelgrass. NDP438.
Ezra Pound, ABC of Reading. NDP89.
  Confucius. NDP285.
  Confucius to Cummings. (Anth.) NDP126.
  Gaudier Brzeska. NDP372.
  Guide to Kulchur. NDP257.
  Literary Essays. NDP250.
  Selected Cantos. NDP304.
  Selected Letters 1907-1941. NDP317.
  Selected Poems. NDP66.
  The Spirit of Romance. NDP266.
  Translations.† (Enlarged Edition) NDP145.
  Women of Trachis. NDP597.
Raymond Queneau, The Blue Flowers. NDP595.
  Exercises in Style. NDP513.
  The Sunday of Life. NDP433.
Mary de Rachewiltz, Ezra Pound. NDP405.
Raja Rao, Kanthapura. NDP224.
Herbert Read, The Green Child. NDP208.
P. Reverdy, Selected Poems.† NDP346.
Kenneth Rexroth, Classics Revisited. NDP621.
  More Classics Revisited, NDP668.
  100 More Poems from the Chinese. NDP308.
  100 More Poems from the Japanese.† NDP420.
  100 Poems from the Chinese. NDP192.
  100 Poems from the Japanese.† NDP147.
  Selected Poems. NDP581.
  Women Poets of China. NDP528.
  Women Poets of Japan. NDP527.
  World Outside the Window, Sel. Essays, NDP639.
Rainer Maria Rilke, Poems from
  The Book of Hours. NDP408.
  Possibility of Being. (Poems). NDP436.
  Where Silence Reigns. (Prose). NDP464.
Arthur Rimbaud, Illuminations.† NDP56.
  Season in Hell & Drunken Boat.† NDP97.
Edouard Roditi, Delights of Turkey. NDP445.

Oscar Wilde. NDP624.
Jerome Rothenberg, New Selected Poems. NDP625.
Nayantara Sahgal, Rich Like Us, NDP665.
Saigyo, Mirror for the Moon.† NDP465.
Ihara Saikaku, The Life of an Amorous
  Woman. NDP270.
St. John of the Cross, Poems.† NDP341.
Jean-Paul Sartre, Nausea. NDP82.
  The Wall (Intimacy). NDP272.
Delmore Schwartz, Selected Poems. NDP241.
  The Ego Is Always at the Wheel, NDP641.
  In Dreams Begin Responsibilities. NDP454.
Stevie Smith, Collected Poems. NDP562.
  New Selected Poems, NDP659.
Gary Snyder, The Back Country. NDP249.
  The Real Work. NDP499.
  Regarding Wave. NDP306.
  Turtle Island. NDP381.
Enid Starkie, Rimbaud. NDP254.
Robert Steiner, Bathers. NDP495.
Antonio Tabucchi, Letter from Casablanca. NDP620.
Nathaniel Tarn, Lyrics . . . Bride of God. NDP391.
Dylan Thomas, Adventures in the Skin Trade.
  NDP183.
  A Child's Christmas in Wales. NDP181.
  Collected Poems 1934-1952. NDP316.
  Collected Stories. NDP626.
  Portrait of the Artist as a Young Dog. NDP51.
  Quite Early One Morning. NDP90.
  Under Milk Wood. NDP73.
Tian Wen: A Chinese Book of Origins. NDP624.
Lionel Trilling, E. M. Forster. NDP189.
Martin Turnell, Baudelaire. NDP336.
  Rise of the French Novel. NDP474.
Paul Valéry, Selected Writings.† NDP184.
Elio Vittorini, A Vittorini Omnibus. NDP366.
Rosmarie Waldrop, The Reproduction of Profiles,
  NDP649.
Robert Penn Warren, At Heaven's Gate. NDP588.
Vernon Watkins, Selected Poems. NDP221.
Weinberger, Eliot, Works on Paper. NDP627.
Nathanael West, Miss Lonelyhearts &
  Day of the Locust. NDP125.
J. Wheelwright, Collected Poems. NDP544.
Tennessee Williams, Camino Real. NDP301.
  Cat on a Hot Tin Roof. NDP398.
  Clothes for a Summer Hotel. NDP556.
  The Glass Menagerie. NDP218.
  Hard Candy. NDP225.
  In the Winter of Cities. NDP154.
  A Lovely Sunday for Creve Coeur. NDP497.
  One Arm & Other Stories. NDP237.
  Stopped Rocking. NDP575.
  A Streetcar Named Desire. NDP501.
  Sweet Bird of Youth. NDP409.
  Twenty-Seven Wagons Full of Cotton. NDP217.
  Vieux Carre. NDP482.
William Carlos Williams,
  The Autobiography. NDP223.
  The Buildup. NDP259.
  The Doctor Stories. NDP585.
  Imaginations. NDP329.
  In the American Grain. NDP53.
  In the Money. NDP240.
  Paterson. Complete. NDP152.
  Pictures form Brueghel. NDP118.
  Selected Letters. NDP589.
  Selected Poems (new ed.). NDP602.
  White Mule. NDP226.
  Yes, Mrs. Williams. NDP534.
Yvor Winters, E. A. Robinson. NDP326.
Wisdom Books: Ancient Egyptians.NDP467.
  Early Buddhists, NDP444; Forest (Hindu).
  NDP414; Spanish Mystics. NDP442; St. Francis.
  NDP477; Taoists. NDP509; Wisdom of the Desert.
  NDP295; Zen Masters. NDP415.

For complete listing request free catalog from
New Directions, 80 Eighth Avenue, New York 10011   † Bilingual